About the author

Michael Hardwick was born in Leeds. Before
joining the Drama Department of the BBC,
he was a Captain in the Indian Army and a
Film Director in New Zealand. Since 1963 he
has been freelancing with his wife, Mollie
Hardwick, and together they have written
over fifty books mainly on literary subjects.
They have also produced a novelization of
Billy Wilder's film *The Private Life of
Sherlock Holmes*. Michael and Mollie
Hardwick live in Highgate Village, London.

Mr. Hudson's Diaries

MICHAEL HARDWICK

SPHERE BOOKS LIMITED
30/32 Gray's Inn Road, London WC1X 8JL

First published in Great Britain
by Sphere Books 1973
Copyright © Sagitta Productions 1973
Reprinted January 1974
Reprinted October 1974

Set in Times Roman

Printed in Great Britain by
Hazell Watson & Viney Ltd
Aylesbury, Bucks

ISBN 0 7221 4304 4

CHAPTER ONE

1 January, 1904

Outside my window a grey winter twilight is beginning to settle on the London roofs. The pavements are glistening with damp, the trees in the gardens of Eaton Square are black and lifeless. Whiles, a shape under an umbrella hurries past the area railings. Through the lace curtains of the Duchess of Knaresborough's drawing-room, on the opposite side of Eaton Place, Her Grace is visible taking tea by the fire, as Lady Marjorie and Mr Bellamy are no doubt doing upstairs, in our own drawing-room.

I am not a man given to melancholy fancies, but I must confess that a certain gloom descended on me after luncheon today. Maybe it was because at this time of year in Scotland there would be an atmosphere of good cheer and merrymaking, even among those who had been celebrating Hogmanay a wee bit too well. Maybe it was this made me the least thing dreich, long though it is since I saw a New Year dawn in Scotland.

Whatever the reason, I found myself turning to a box of papers I have had by me, unopened, since the first week of my coming to this house. It is not my way to hoard, and the space in my room is not great, but there were things in the box I had promised myself to look at one day. A butler's life in a household such as ours is a busy one, and the day had never come, until this afternoon. I took the box from my wardrobe cupboard (it was not locked, for our staff are trustworthy) and opened it, laying out its contents, one by one, upon my table.

The photographs. My Mother, with her gentle

pretty face, her tiny waist and bell-shaped crinoline skirt of black silk, her very best, holding the baby that was me in her arms, against a very grand balustrade made of cardboard which the photographer used as a background for his sitters; and my Father, standing beside her tall and proud, in his fine Sunday suit with the high collar. You can see the shine of his sandy-gold curls and luxuriant whiskers (I take my colouring from him) even in the faded old picture. 'John Mac-farren, photographer, Glasgow' reads the advertisement on the back. They had taken me all the way to Glasgow from our home in Garbeg, at the head of Loch Lomond, for in those days there were no cameras in the homes of gamekeepers.

My Grandmother, in her lace cap with the lappets. Very stern and proud she looks (and indeed, pride was to be her death). She had been a Mackenzie of the Isles: Morag Mackenzie, a daughter of the clan that was aye loyal to the Stuarts even when German George set a price of £3000 on Prince Charlie's head to tempt his followers. She was never tired of telling us children tales of the 'Forty-five. I see her now in my mind's eye, not grim as she seems in her portrait, but all afire with the drama of her story, her Highland voice lilting triumphantly or sinking to an awesome whisper. Her favourite tale, and ours, was that of Roderick Mackenzie who had been 'out' in the 'Forty-five, and played a nobly tragic part.

'He was my Grandfather,' she would tell us (who knew it perfectly well) 'for I was born in '88, the very year our Prince died far away in Rome. Only the two generations between you and Roderick, Angus! And he was the bonniest of all our family, a man of six feet and more, his hair as yellow as the sun and as long as a lassie's, his eyes of the peat-brown. I have the very same myself.' And she would widen her own fine dark eyes to prove it.

'Not only this, bairns, but, forbye—*Roderick was*

6

the very image of the Bonnie Prince! And so, being brave as a lion and caring nothing for his own skin, when the troops of Butcher Cumberland were mowing down our Highland men at the bloody battle of Culloden, Roderick Mackenzie threw himself into the heart of the fight, in the hope that the English might capture or kill him, taking him for Prince Charlie. Aye, and so they did, and with his last breath he cried to them "Ye have slain your Prince!" '

Then she would tell us of the Prince's escape, and his long hiding in the hills. I can hear her now, looking on her face, sharp as a mountain eagle's . . . But I digress. My Grandfather's picture is beside hers. All there is to say of him is not said in a moment. Later, I will write what I recall of that strange, wild man. Now I am remembering the childhood of my Sister and Brother from their likenesses: Donald, two years my junior, at five, sturdy and fair, gazing earnestly at the photographer as though thinking out the answer to some deep question, while baby Fiona leans against his knee laughing, a frilled bonnet askew on her curls, her chubby legs button-booted.

Here is myself, seven-year-old Angus, a lanky serious lad, standing stiffly straight beside a table with an aspidistra on it. I remember well the day at Dumbarton: how the man with his head hidden under the black cloth made daft chirping noises and snapped his fingers, trying to get a wee smile out of me, and how I felt it was a very solemn occasion on which I must look as sober as a wet Sabbath morn.

Beneath the photographs I found a pile of notebooks. My diaries: the life of Angus Roderick Hudson from a boy to a young man. Something in me held back from opening them. Which of us can look back on his life, scene after scene passing before his eyes, without regret for many a wrong turn taken, for chances missed? Even the happy moments are little but pleasant dreams only half-remembered, as the greatest Scotsman of us all has written:

'But pleasures are like poppies spread,
You seize the flower, its bloom is shed.'

It was just at this moment that a tap on my door announced Mrs Bridges, our cook. Having missed me from the tea-table the good soul had brought me a tray of tea, sandwiches and cakes.

'For there's no sense in neglecting yourself, Mr Hudson,' she said, 'even if you're a bit down in the mouth, as I can see you are.'

Mrs Bridges and I have been in service together for over twenty years. I have the highest respect for her integrity and level-headedness; so I did not hesitate to make her my confidante (and in any case she had already noticed the little collection of relics covering my table, and was inspecting them over my shoulder.)

'I'll tell you what it is,' she declared, when I had come to the end of my somewhat lame account of my feelings, 'A man that can't face his past is a poor sort of creature, and that, Mr Hudson, in my opinion you are *not*. Now if you'll take my advice you'll have your tea and then sit down and go through all them old books of yours. And if you don't end up feeling you've been luckier than most and have a sight less to be ashamed of, my name's Queen Alexandra, God bless her.'

She poured me a cup of steaming tea with the three lumps of sugar she knows I take. Gratefully I sipped it.

'Mrs Bridges,' I said, 'as ever, your judgment is excellent. Tonight the Family are dining elsewhere. I will take the rare opportunity of a leisure hour or two to peruse my diaries.'

'Why don't you start a new one?' she asked, on her way out. 'It would take your mind off things.'

The remark recalled me to my duties. 'I heard a crash just now', I said. 'Has Emily by any chance broken another piece of crockery?'

Mrs Bridges sniffed. 'It wasn't Emily this time, it was Sarah, dancing about to make them others laugh, and it was my favourite jug with the roses on she knocked off the dresser into smithereens. It'll be stopped out of her wages, if you'll take my advice.'

'I usually do take your advice, Mrs Bridges,' I replied with a smile. 'For example, I am greatly enjoying the tea you kindly provided, and I shall afterwards settle down to the perusal of my diaries.'

When she had left, I finished the last of her excellent Coburg cakes and settled to my papers. First I turned up the lamp and put on my spectacles. Perhaps it is a sign of advancing age that I find I cannot dispense with them except when reading the largest print. Happily my duties do not oblige me to wear them constantly, and I believe they impress the younger servants. I added another lump of coal to the fire which I am fortunate enough to have in my bedroom, and in the cheerful blaze and the yellow rays of the brightened lamp I opened the first volume.

10 September, 1866

Today is my birthday. I am ten years old. My name is Angus Roderick Hudson. I am going to write down things about myself because I intend to become a famous man and so it is my duty.

My Father is Ian Charles Hudson and he is gamekeeper to Lord Invermore and we live in a cottage on Lord Invermore's estate which is by the shore of Loch Lomond. The nearest village to us is Garbeg. My Grandfather's name is Robert Hudson and he was born in Glasgow which is a great city some miles away on the River Clyde. I have been to Glasgow twice and I found it very impressive.

My brother Donald is two years younger than me

and is very clever. He is top of the school in mathematics and our Dominie, Mr Blair, says he will become a grand engineer. He can draw very fine designs for buildings and machines.

I am also clever though the Minister says I am inclined to the sin of pride and must learn humility. But Father says 'Speak the truth and shame the De'il' and therefore I must confess that I am clever. When I become a man I shall be a great Advocate.

I put down the diary. How well I recall that second visit to Glasgow (even at the arrogant age of ten I could hardly claim to remember the first, the occasion of my infant likeness being taken.) But the second!

It was my Grandfather who took me, to a session of the Assizes. He had a keen interest in criminal matters, long before novels of detection came into fashion as popular reading. There were some in Garbeg who said that it was because he would have made a great criminal himself. (Again I long to digress, but I must return to my memories.)

I sat, very small and awed, on a hard bench in a crowded courtroom. My Grandfather sat beside me; he had been told to extinguish his pipe by an official at the door, and in consequence was in a bad humour. But I was all eyes and ears. A man was being tried for murder. His name was Alastair Snow, a tailor, a thin little man who clung to the edge of the dock as though he were drowning and it were the edge of a boat. We were quite near, and I could see beads of sweat trickling from his black hair and coursing down his face. I felt deeply sorry for him, as sorry as for a rabbit caught in one of my father's traps; but from my Grandfather's murmured commentary and remarks around us something penetrated to my mind to the effect that he was a man of sinful life and deserved to die, whether he had killed the woman or not.

'Whoring after strange flesh,' remarked my Grandfather, with satisfaction. He appeared to be enjoying the trial, after his first sulkiness at being deprived of his pipe, rather in the manner in which people today enjoy the Bioscope. (I myself prefer a seat at the theatre, which these modern inventions will surely never supersede.)

A great deal was said about a quarrel overheard between Snow and the woman, and his subsequent flight from the tenement in which they lived. A man in a wig, with an English accent, made a long speech, often pointing his finger at the prisoner and raising his voice to a shout. The crowd began to rustle excitely. 'It's the gallows!' my Grandfather exclaimed gleefully. 'He'll swing, sure as daith!' and the people surrounding us were saying the like. A court official cried out to them to keep silent. In the great carved chair under the Royal arms an old man whom my Grandfather said was the Judge sat huddled like a toad, sometimes writing a few words, sometimes appearing to be asleep.

I do not remember noticing when a man whom my Grandfather called the Counsel for the Defence got up and began to speak. He was young and rather colourless, less impressive in his grey curled wig than the others who had spoken. Then I began to listen, for I was carried away by the force and fervour of his words, though of course I could not have described my feelings at the time except as those of boyish admiration. Our Minister, I felt, was trying to be like this young Mr McLachlan when he shouted and groaned at us from the pulpit on the Sabbath about what deadly sinners we were, but he had no such power.

I wish I could see in print that young man's speech. Phrases drift back to me: 'Improper evidence based on irrelevancies', 'Judge not, that ye be not judged', these were among them. What of the woman victim?

11

he said. She was of notorious character and had other associates whose evidence of her looseness of life had been heard, and others doubtless existed as capable of committing the crime as the prisoner in the dock. More and more convincing and impassioned grew the young advocate until the whole courtroom was hanging on his words. Still in my middle-aged ears rings the last sentence of his appeal.

'Above His Lordship's head, gentlemen, you behold the Royal Arms of Scotland. As you look upon that noble emblem, let me remind you of another and nobler attribute of Royalty; let me point out to you the brightest jewel in Her Majesty's crown. What, may you ask, is that jewel? Gentlemen, it is Mercy.'

The effect of Mr McLachlan's speech upon the jury was electric. And when the verdict was returned, it was one of Not Proven, that ambiguous phrase of Scots law which indicates that insufficient evidence exists for a conviction. I have never seen a face so transformed as that of the rabbit-like little creature in the dock, as the shadow of Death passed from above his head; and, from that moment, no hero of my childhood could equal that young advocate.

I have told this story at length to remind myself of what I was at that time. Ambition had taken a firm root in my mind, I was an eager pupil for the education which Scotland is proud to give her humblest children, and which they are quick to take from her. Little did I know what the future held for me.

I turned over the old pages again.

16 August, 1867

Queen Victoria has been on the throne thirty years and six months. Today there was a great shoot, over 400 birds Father said. I was glad I had to go to school and not with the beaters which Father makes me do when there is a holiday. The birds are so bonnie I do not like to see them fall. One day I asked Lord Invermore when he came to our cottage why Father had to look after the hens and chicks all the Spring and Summer so that they could be shot in the Autumn. Mother said 'Wheesht, Angus!' and Father said 'Dinna ask sic a daft question of his Lordship!' and looked angry. But Lord Invermore laughed and said it was a very good question and he supposed the answer was that the slaughter of grouse and ptarmigan provided sport for the House of Lords who might otherwise have been tempted to sit through the Recess. Then Mother said quickly it was not just that. Lady Invermore kindly sent presents of game to all the tenantry and especially those in our countryside who were poor.

When Lord Invermore had gone I heard Father saying to Mother: 'Whiles, Margaret, I fear our Angus will grow tae be a richt jessie. Did ye ever hear the like? "Why should the birds be shot?" he says.' And Mother's soft voice said 'Angus has a kind hairt, Ian, no' a saft heid. There's a wheen difference.' I could not see her but I knew that she had laid her hand upon his arm and she was looking up at him in the way that always makes him smile even when he is displeased. My Mother is very pretty and has eyes like the roe-deer they stalk up in Glen Fyne. I do not like to see the deer shot, indeed I cannot watch them die. But I shall not mention this to Father.

I sighed reminiscently. I must have been the most inappropriate son ever to be born to a gamekeeper, even to one as good-hearted and gentle-handed as my Father. I loved to go with him on his rounds of the breeding birds and to see his care of them and their young, but it turned me sick to see the limp corpses of stoats and squirrels, weasels, rats nailed cruelly to the doors of sheds, 'as a warning tae the rest', said my Father. I could not see how such simple beasts could have the power of reasoning thus, nor how men like my Father and the underkeepers who sang solemn

13

hymns about the crucifixion of our Lord in the Kirk could bring themselves to crucify his creatures or torture them to die in steel-clawed traps. My only comfort was to remember that it was the duty of Lord Invermore's keepers to protect his game. I see this even more clearly now.

But there are many happy memories in my first diaries. How Donald and I would take our food and our fishing-rods, and set off early on a holiday morning away to the loch-side. There we two laddies would bide all day, talking or silent. Across the loch Ben Lomond reared his great head, his slopes purple with heather and golden-bronze with Autumn foliage, and beyond him to the north stretched the mountains that bordered Glen Falloch, dreaming beneath the changing sky that turned Loch Lomond's water to a great opal.

Dear me, I am waxing poetical. I thought such things had been left behind with my youth. And I see, on looking back at these few pages, that I am drifting into the Scots way of talk of those far-off days; I that have lived in England so many years, and flatter myself that my speech is as pure and precise in its way as that of Mr Bellamy himself. It is all one, this harking-back, to the vividness with which I recall those golden sunlit days, the scent of the heather and the rich mountain air, the pleasure of my Mother when we returned home with our catch; the aroma of the fish cooking, the sight of it fine and fresh on our plates as we sat round the table. First Father would stand to say Grace, then he would take wee Fiona on his knee and feed her with scraps, for of all of us she was his darling.

What is this?

Today we held a trial. Jimmy McNab was the accused and I was Prosecuting Counsel. Donald spoke for the defence but he found little to say and I rebuked him for laughing in court and turned him out.

Then I became the Judge and sentenced Jimmy to ten years in gaol, though I could not well hear myself speak because Donald was outbye singing 'Wha saw the Forty-second, Wha saw the Forty-twa, Wha saw the Forty-Second, Marching doon the Broomielaw.' Jimmy did not like being sentenced and I told him not to greet like a wee bairn.

Well, well, these are childish things. Here I find an occasion worth recording.

29 September, 1869
A great event is going to happen. Queen Victoria is coming to visit at the Castle! . . .

I was about to read on, but stirrings in the kitchen warn me that it is supper-time. I close my book with a strange regret, and a resolve; from time to time I will set aside a few moments from my duties to continue my perusal of my old journals and the writing of this, my new one.

CHAPTER TWO

How it came about that Her Majesty paid a visit to Invermore Castle I cannot at this date remember. Perhaps I never knew. The estate in Dumbartonshire lay many miles to the south and west of Balmoral in Aberdeenshire, where the Queen spent many of her Summers and Autumns. Lord Invermore, though a Tory peer and therefore in Her Majesty's good books as a supporter of her beloved Disraeli, played little part in political affairs and found London life disagreeable, as I once heard him tell my Father. Yet for some reason Her Majesty decided to honour his Castle with a visit, travelling far out of her way back to Windsor in order to do so.

Wild excitement ruled our community, of course. I read in my diary for 3 October:

Everyone is hanging out flags and putting loyal greetings in their windows. They say it is the same all through the shire, from Ardlui to Balloch. Fiona has drawn a picture of the Queen, after the one we have in the parlour, though I fear it is somewhat out of date as it shows her at the age of nineteen, whereas this year she is fifty. Mr Kelso the bookseller has bought some copies of her book, *Leaves from the Journal of our Life in the Highlands,* and they are displayed in his shop window, bound very elegant in green leather, though very few can afford to buy one. The Castle gates have great banners draped over them in red, white and blue, inscribed with *God Save our Gracious Queen* and *Long May She Reign.* Lady Invermore has had a cart-load of flowers sent up from Glasgow. I hope it will be a fine day tomorrow:

Donald and I think it will be, from the sunset this evening.

My Brother and I were for once incorrect weather-prophets. On the day of the Queen's arrival it rained as it can rain only in Scotland. Grey sheets of water obscured the hills and the glens, rivers flowed down the gutters of the village street. The banners on the Castle gates became limp rags, the colours running into one another. Deer and cattle huddled under trees, as gloomy as the human faces which peered through streaming window-panes at the route the Queen would take. Yet, undeterred, as the hour approached when the Royal coach might be expected to appear, the people emerged from houses and cottages and converged on the Castle. Lord Invermore had given his permission for them to line the drive from the gates to the Castle entrance, providing they were in place in good time, not to interfere with Her Majesty's progress.

My Grandparents had walked all the way from Porthulish, where Grandfather worked in the Excise-house. Mother, Grandmother and Fiona lamented in chorus the extinguishing of their best bonnets and cloaks beneath disfiguring macintoshes and black umbrellas. Fiona was deeply distressed about the ruin of her black ringlets, specially curled for the occasion.

'I didna get a wink of sleep for the curlpapers!' she wailed. 'They stickit into my heid like knives, and look at me now!'

'*She*'ll ha'e mair to do than admire your hair,' said Mother; but I noted that she had carefully adjusted to the most becoming angle a little hat which had drawn censorious glances from the pulpit, the Reverend Gentleman evidently disapproving of the small bunch of artificial wheat and poppies adorning it.

Grandmother had pinned her cameo brooch to the high neck of her best dress, a black, rusty with long wear. Varying expressions flitted across her mobile

17

face, for her attitude to this occasion was a mixture of indignation that the German Woman, one of the usurping Hanoverian line, should be considered welcome in Scotland, and sheer female curiosity allied to a determination not to miss anything. Both Grandfather and Father were in their stiff best suits, also black; we were sober-clad folk in those days. I was wearing mine, but with discomfort, being at that agonizing stage of a boy's growth when his wrists protrude from his sleeves and his ankles from his trousers, and yet there is no money for new clothes. Donald, being shorter, appeared altogether more seemly.

So together we set out to secure a good place by the gates; and stood heroically with our neighbours in a torrential downpour. A sudden ripple of excitement ran through the ranks as those near the end of the drive began to cheer. A piper, his kilt and plaid of Macgregor tartan sodden, even his pipes black with rain, began to play the Pibroch of Donuil Dhu, and his martial strains whipped our expectations to fever height.

Then the Royal coach came into view. I leave it to my young self to describe the scene:

Mother's umbrella almost put out my eye, but I managed to see everything. The carriage was going very slowly and it was an open one, which surprised everybody, but Father was later told that the Queen insisted on this so that her people might see her without obstruction. A wee umbrella was all she had to keep off the rain. I had heard that since Prince Albert's death she dressed entirely in black, but she wore a bonnet with brown and yellow feathers on it. I was surprised to see her so small and fat and not at all like Fiona's picture, with a beaky nose and no shape at all so far as could be told. I was also surprised that she smiled so cheerfully, bowing from side to side, but this it seems was because she is happiest

18

when in the Highlands and thinks of Balmoral Castle as her home even more than Windsor.

I felt tears come to my eyes, nor was I the only one to betray unmanly emotion. Our folks are not given to such displays, but even such lang-faced loons as Andy Drum were cheering and skirling enough to drown the pipes. I took a sideways keek at Grandmother and saw that she was laughing and greeting at once and shouting something in the Gaelic.

'Whaur's your Prince Charlie noo?' I whispered to her, and got a sharp smack on the hand for my pains.

As the coach moved up the drive we all followed it, until it reached the Castle doorway. There it stopped to await the coming of another carriage, a closed one. From this a man descended, big, rough-looking, bearded, and wearing the kilt. He strode to the Queen's carriage before anyone else could approach it, and unceremoniously took her hand and pulled rather than assisted her to the ground. I saw his lips move and noted an expression of surprise, even horror, on the faces of Lord and Lady Invermore, who awaited their Royal visitor beneath the porch.

Afterwards a crony of Mother's from the Castle household told us what the man had said.

'Ye'll no' credit it,' said Elspeth. 'I dinna masel', though I heard it as plain as you hear me. He said "Hoots, wumman, could ye no' haud yer umbrella up and keep your dommed bonnet dry?"'

We gasped. Elspeth continued, 'They say his name's John Broon and he's the Queen's Highland Servant, for all that he was only a ghillie when Prince Albert was alive. And they say he takes *liberties*.'

'No!' Mother was suitably scandalised.

'Aye' Elspeth lowered her voice. 'He gangs tae her bedroom when she's no' even dressed. And they do say—'

To my disappointment Mother requested me to leave the room at this point, but it was not long before I heard from the talk of my schoolmates that John Brown was rumoured to have an illicit relationship with the Queen. I found this not only shocking but difficult to believe. Her Majesty is both dignified and amiable, but by no means handsome.

Tonight there is to be free ale and whisky for all the male tenants in the Castle kitchens. I am afraid Grandfather will get drunk again.

I closed the diary. Even at this date I can scarcely credit the freedom of John Brown's speech and manner before Her Majesty. When I recall how Mr Bellamy, a kind and considerate master, dismissed instantly a young footman for some unseemly remark in Lady Marjorie's presence, I can see clearly that the scandalous rumours concerning the Queen and Brown were, in fact, Her Majesty's fault. A servant, however trusted and confidential, must never take advantage of that trust and confidence. I have recently noted a tendency in Alfred to make undesirably eccentric observations in the hearing of the maids, verging on the offensive. If I discover him seriously upsetting Rose or Emily I shall be obliged to report him to Mr Bellamy. I do not anticipate his upsetting Sarah, as I overheard her countering some sally of his with the music-hall ballad 'Oh, George, don't you think you're going Just a Bit too Far?'

My mind strays back to the past. That first night of the Royal visit produced some sore heads the morning after, thanks to His Lordship's generosity in the distribution of liquors. Father came home merry, but 'far frae fou', as Mother approvingly observed. The same could not be said of Grandfather, who did not come home at all, but was discovered next day by one of the Castle farm-workers, with two empty whisky-bottles in his pockets, in a disused pig-sty. Grandmother, who had spent the night at our house, said grimly that it was just the place in which one might expect to find him.

I see I have not recorded this episode in my diary. Grandfather's lapses were infrequent and always followed the same pattern. I remember them from when I was only a wee boy, but it was not until many years later that I understood their nature.

There is, I believe, some term in this new German science of psychology which describes those who are within themselves two totally different people. Such a man was my Grandfather. In Porthulish he was a sober, douce man, a conscientious worker in the Excise-office and not unpopular, considering the highly unpopular nature of his occupation. He allowed generous housekeeping money to Grandmother, travelled the long miles between their home and ours for family celebrations and at other times, and showed us a restrained affection. If I did not admire him as I did my lively Grandmother it was because he gave no cause for admiration: he had no thrilling tales to tell, no trophies to show. I would have described him as dour if that word did not connote a certain ill-temper.

He lived a life of clockwork, journeying to his office every day on foot from the cottage set high on a hillside, and returning every day at the same time. Then, after supper, it was his custom to sit in a somewhat uncomfortable chair by the fire, reading, while Grandmother, who could never sit still for long, jumped up every few minutes to brew some tea òr fetch a garment to sew; anything to employ her time. When I went to their cottage in an evening, as I sometimes did with Father, I felt I should keep very quiet, as still as a mouse, not to disturb Grandfather's reading. But Grandmother had no such inhibitions. She flitted about singing or humming, chattering to us or to herself, and answering herself back.

I knew this dull life must be far from her inclination, and one night, indeed, I caught her gaze dwelling thoughtfully on the silent figure by the fire, while she knitted and hummed a tune. I recognised the tune: *Breigein Binneach*, a Gaelic song of a girl promised a fine house by her husband-to-be, but finding it only a miserable hut.

She caught me looking at her, and, her eyes smiling, laid her finger across her lips for a second in warning.

But one evening, when Grandfather had gone to bed early with a fearsome cold, I said to her, 'Is it no' terrible lonely for you here, Nannie, without a word spoken to you and no neighbours near?'

She looked at me with an expression my boyish mind could make nothing of, before saying, 'I am glad to have him at home, Angus.'

That was all. I must have been seven or eight when I knew the truth behind that sentence. Every five weeks, or so, sometimes more often, Grandfather would rise from his chair, put down his book with the place carefully marked by a Sunday-school Bible bookmarker, don his outdoor clothes and take his crooked stick from the corner. At the door he would turn and say to Grandmother, 'I'll be awa' noo.'

And out he would go, returning perhaps a week later to resume his routine as if he had never been absent.

When this first happened, it distressed his wife sorely. Thoughts of him associating with thieves, co-habiting with another woman, taking refuge in a mad-house from some recurrent demon of the brain, chased each other round her distracted head. The absences had begun after the birth late in her marriage of her two children, my Father and Aunt Ailie. She was alone with them, a baby and a toddler, in that bleak spot with the nearest human dwelling half a mile away down the steep path. After the third absence, and her complete failure to get a word on the subject out of Grandfather, she decided on an extraordinary means of solving the mystery.

22

She had Grandfather followed.

There was no such thing as a Private Detective in those days — or none that I know of. The person she went to for help was Willie Allan. Nobody knew what Willie did for a living; certainly he had no local work. I have learnt since that he lived entirely by odd jobs, working in the Clyde shipyards, shepherding up at Inverary, jobbing on road-works along with the Paddies. He was a man of some thirty years or so, though he might well have been younger, with a pleasant enough but undistinguished face. He might be found anywhere in the district, as unpredictable in his habits as Grandfather, in his normal state, was predictable. He knew everybody's business: 'If you want to ken what yer ain mither's thinking, ask Willie,' people said.

When Willie heard Grandmother's story, he stroked his chin.

'So he winna tell you whaur he goes. Well, neither a coax or a squeeze can get an egg oot of a sweer hen. When d'ye expect the neist turn?'

She told him it would be almost certainly within the next week, for he had been at home now for six, the longest interval so far. Willie scanned the bright June sky.

'It stays licht till nine. When he's awa', stand in the doorway and wave yon red shawl. I'll be at the ben-foot when he gets there.'

'And follow him?'

'Tae the far places of the earth for you, Mistress Morag,' Willie said with an admiring glance. 'And I'll just tak' a kiss on account.' Which, my Grandmother told me, blushing even at her age, he did.

I will summarise the rambling and colourful story Willie brought back to her a few hours before Grandfather's return. The beginning of his journey had led him to one of the least reputable inns in the district. Here Grandfather took four drams of whisky and bought a bottle to carry away. Willie, who had unobtrusively refreshed himself with ale, dogged his footsteps from the inn down the road which leads from Porthulish so far that Willie began to fear his prey was heading for Glasgow.

But at Helensburgh (a fitting place with a great distillery) Grandfather left the road and scrambled down the bank to the shore. There was a small, rough cottage, with a few boats in front of it on the shingle. Grandfather went to the door and knocked loudly on it. Willie saw that it was a man who answered the door and let Grandfather in. The door immediately shut again, and Willie sat down to wait. He waited five hours.

'Five hours! By the loch!' exclaimed Grandmother in horror.

'Och, we Allans are no' killed easy. I was wrappit in ma plaid and I had a drappie of Glenlivet in ma flask,' Willie said airily.

At four o'clock the next morning, as dawn broke, the two men came out of the cottage, dragged the largest of the boats down to the water, got in it and rowed away. Willie, who had never expected such a manoeuvre, stared after them helplessly. They were bound due south; but bound whither? Possibly Gourock, on the opposite bank of the upper reach of the Clyde; possibly along the west coast down to somewhere in Ayrshire; possibly America, thought Willie with bitterness.

He was no sneakthief to enter a house without welcome, but he went to the door of the bothy and pushed. It was unlocked, and he went in. It was a one-roomed place, and that room bare and chill. Blankets on the floor showed where the men had slept, and there was evidence of porridge having been made and kippers grilled on the fire, and of the fire having been extinguished. No clues anywhere.

Then Willie's sharp eyes caught sight of a map

24

open on the table. It was a large section map, showing the area of sea, islands, and coast, from the place where he was to the end of the Firth of Clyde. He would have learnt nothing from it if he had not noticed on the dull red of the Isle of Arran a brighter red circle drawn round a place-name. It was on the north-east side of Arran, and the place was Corrie.

The odds were against him, but Willie Allan believed in intuition. Darting back to the road, he walked briskly down to Balloch, the next village, where he found a small boat-yard with a proprietor willing to take him across the Clyde to Cardross.

From Cardross he walked to Port Glasgow, and there got taken as a casual hand on a merchant-ship sailing that night for Campbeltown, Kintyre. By morning the busy Glasgow coast had been left behind. Ahead, to the south-west, lay the Isle of Arran.

Willie later told my Grandmother that he had no doubts by that time but that his instinct was right, and that he would find his man at Corrie. 'I hae but a wee drap o' Highland bluid, but it stands me in guid stead,' he said with pride.

At Corrie they put him ashore and paid him what he had earned on the voyage. And that fine June day he found my Grandfather, though my Grandfather never glimpsed a whisker of him, for Willie was one had the strange gift of making himself invisible, like a woodland beast.

My Grandfather, he said, was living in a shepherd's hut, in a wild place carpeted with honey-scented thyme and heather on the slopes of Goat Fell, that looming height which some call The Old Man, for from a certain point it seems like the outline of a sleeping giant. Outside the hut a pile of ashes and twigs laid on stones marked the remains of a bush-fire which Willie guessed would be lit at night when the evening chill came down, and it was time for supper.

As Willie took his sights of the spot, a human sound

25

disturbed birds perching in a tree nearby. Willie dodged behind a boulder and froze, as one who earns part of his daily bread by catching his own food knows now to freeze, silent and unseen. From a clump of firs below came Grandfather.

On one shoulder was a gun; on the other a brace of rabbits tied together. Blood from them dripped down Grandfather's coat, which was not the coat he wore at Porthulish, but a rough frieze garment which Willie could almost smell from behind his rock. Grandfather's nether regions were covered by tartan trews of great age and filthiness. As he came up the hill he sang, and Willie listened incredulously.

For Grandfather was singing *John Anderson, my jo, John*. What could be more innocent? But, in fact, it was the old version which he sang; a version well known to our great Rabbie before he wrote the new one. I find it hard to confide even to my diary the words of this song, but broadly speaking it was the lament of an auld wife, not for her John's baldness but for his — how can I express it? — his loss of virility. As the verses grew increasingly shocking Grandfather's face broke into a broad grin. There, thought Willie to himself, goes a happy man.

My Grandfather marched up to the hut, slung the rabbits and the gun on the ground and entered his wild habitation. And then came the thing which Willie would never tell Grandmother, but told me when I had come to years of discretion. 'Angus,' he said, 'I dinna ken how ye'll tak' this, but. . .'

At that point my dream of the past is rudely shattered. Rose has appeared at my door to tell me that Emily is having hysterics brought on by the appearance of some cockroaches from under the boiler. These interruptions are most annoying: I begin to fancy myself a literary man, not to be disturbed until the Muse has forsaken me. Reluctantly I lay down my pen until a more auspicious occasion.

26

CHAPTER THREE

All is calm again. The cockroaches have been routed, and Emily restored with the aid of burnt feathers. My lamplit room in Eaton Place has vanished in the mists, and I am once more sitting outside a small tavern, as Willie Allan tells me the end of his tale.

As my Grandfather entered the bothy, still singing his bawdy song, Willie in the shadow of the boulder saw someone come out to meet him. It was a girl, a slip of a lass, yet with a knowing look in her eyes and an insolent swing to her hips. Her hair and her eyes were black as night, her skin dusky-gold; round her neck hung a circlet of pierced coins. She was, no mistake, a gipsy, one of the roving kind. And my Grandfather seized her in a bearlike embrace, kissing her more as if he had intentions on her life than her person.

Willie could not bring himself to be a spy. He slipped from out of the shadow of the rock and silently made his way down the hillside. At the inn, down in Corrie, he learnt by judicious questions that a stranger came there at intervals, and had been seen up at Lorsa Water, fishing, and trapping game up near Lochranza and elsewhere. They were not concerned in other folks' business in Corrie. The stranger might well be a mad Englishman, or an eccentric from Glasgow. Willie finished his drink and left, travelling back by steamer and taking a two-three days over the journey.

He told Grandmother everything but the last part of the tale. There was, as he said, just that touch of the Highlander in him to perceive that while she might accept my Grandfather's strange return to Nature, her pride would never admit of a rival. She was, said

Willie in a burst of lyricism over his third stoup of whisky, like unto the great and proud Montrose addressing his country:

> 'For if Committees thou erect,
>   Or parties by the score,
> I'll dance and sing at thy neglect,
>   And never love thee more.'

Willie and I looked significantly at each other. I was almost a man, in my own estimation, and flattered myself (erroneously, alas) that I knew something of women.

'I ken fine what you mean, Willie,' I said. 'Did she speir at ye at all, as if she guessed there was a wumman in the case?'

'Nae sic thing. She seemed glad aboot the ither matters, and said, "A wild Scot is the wildest of a' beasts. While Robert can live wild awa' he'll bide quiet at hame." '

But with this I am leaping into the future, after Grandfather's lapses from grace had brought sorrow on our house.

I pick up my diary for the year 1870, after the echoes of Her Majesty's visit had died down. (Dear me, how obscured my spectacles are. I feel this London fog seeping in through every window cranny and down every chimney.) Here I am in April, 1870:

Mr. Kelso called me in today and said he had a book for me. Part of the covers was missing and he could not have sold it well, so he kindly presented me with it. I was maybe a wee bit cast down when I saw the title: it was *Tools and Machinery*, by James Nasmith, inventor of the steam-hammer. But I thanked Mr Kelso for his kind thought, and took the book home to Donald. He is the one to make good use of it.

The Dominie says Donald will be a great engineer some day, but he is too fond of his logarithms and neglects the other lessons for them. I shall set aside an hour every evening to teaching him.

Dear me. What a cocksure lad I was! Donald might have a weakness in his studies, but Angus, never. Angus was to be the greatest of all advocates, judging his fellow-men from the Seats of the Mighty. Just how this wonderful state was to be brought about, I never considered. I was doing nothing towards it myself. Maybe I should have begged a read of law-books or the lives of famous lawyers from Mr Kelso. But it never occurred to me, so sure was I that I would one day don the wig and gown and become the figure of my dreams in a moment.

Meanwhile I read avidly. Our books at home consisted of the Holy Bible, the works of Burns and Shakespeare, Sir Walter Scott's poems, and his book *The Heart of Midlothian.* Dazzled by the last, I set about to borrow Sir Walter's other books from the Dominie and Mr Kelso. On Winter nights I would sit in the inglenook reading by the light of our precious oil-lamp. Summer found me roaming the glens, a book and some bannocks and a slice of cheese in my pack. My imagination was born. I was Guy Mannering, Montrose, Ivanhoe (for which heroic character I had to carry my mind across the Border into unknown England). I was Marmion, taking revenge on those who had walled up his beloved Constance alive; Rob Roy leading Clan Alpine against their oppressors. I lived in a land of noble deeds and aery fantasies.

My Mother sighed at the sight of me with a book propped up against the teapot, dropping food from my fork onto the floor, so intent was I on the page. She knew that if she took it away from me I would only read the label on the marmalade-jar.

I read the newspapers, of course, walking into

Garbeg once a week to Mr Kelso's reading-room. In that year of 1870 a terrible war broke out between France and Prussia. With horror I learned that the citizens of besieged Paris were eating cats, dogs, and even rats, to keep alive. Noble Garibaldi came to their aid; Rome joined the new Kingdom of Italy.

In June the great Charles Dickens died. Remote as we were among our mountains, we had heard of him — the Dominie had even read a few of his works, though novels were generally looked on with suspicion by the Kirk Elders, and I doubt if even Mr Blair would have cared to be caught reading one. It seems strange to think that our maids today spend much of their Sabbath leisure time with their noses in penny novel-ettes without drawing a reproof from me or Mrs. Bridges. Times have changed indeed, and not always for the worse, I must admit, as I recall those dreich Sabbaths when there was nothing to do but go to the Kirk and come back, and the only reading permitted was the Bible. My Father was not a drinking man, but he aye liked his dram of an evening and we bairns could see that he was not entirely himself without it, or Mother entirely herself without a piece of sewing in her hand.

But to return to our reading material. Donald cared less for news of wars abroad than for anything to do with new inventions. I well remember his excited face at the tidings that ferro-concrete buildings had been perfected, and his exasperation that I was unable to share in his exhilaration.

'D'ye no' see,' I hear him saying, 'the whole beauty of it lies in the equality of the coefficients of expansion and the distribution of stresses caused by the welding of two elements?'

'No,' I said.

He shook his head in disbelief. 'That a brither of mine shouldna understand a simple thing. . . I'll build a fine bridge one day, just to show.'

And now he has, and I — but that path leads no-where. I turn over to another page of my diary for 1870:

I am fourteen years old today. Yesterday I walked Jessie Lukar home from the Kirk.

Jessie Lukar! The very name brings back her face to me more clearly than my own in yon mirror by the washbasin. Curly-haired, dark and dimpling was Jessie, the greatest flirt in Dumbartonshire, though not yet twelve. Her father was one of Lord Invermore's gardeners, living in a cottage like ours to the south of the Castle. How many hours did I spend lurking in that vicinity, hoping to see Jessie returning from school; in my pocket there would be a present for her, a witchy marble alluringly striped, a rare stone from the loch-shore, a boiled sweet. Once, in a fury of devotion, I tried to turn the claw of a grouse brought home by Father into the kind of ornamental brooch worn by ladies. In the absence of a silver mount, and of the slightest skill on my part, the result was gruesome indeed.

'Och, awa'!' exclaimed Jessie when I bashfully held the offering out to her. 'If I wanted a deid bird's fuit I'd ask ma Daddie. Onyway, it's high.' She elevated her charming nose. I sniffed; reluctantly I had to admit that it was.

What motive, other than blind Nature, guided my pursuit of Jessie, I cannot say. We were both children, more innocent than are today's, yet she was old enough to flirt and I to gaze. Perhaps she was the nearest thing I had to Ivanhoe's Rebecca, to dashing Di Vernon and Ellen of the Lake. I may have had some dim idea of marrying her one day, though even I, simpleton that I was, knew that early marriage was not for people in our walk of life. A man must be established in his own trade first, before taking a wife, or the bairns would go breadless.

I brooded on the verses of the immortal lover, Rabbie Burns, who seemed to have a lot of Jessies among his fancies: the Flower o' Dunblane, and the lassie of one of his sweetest songs, which I would hum tunelessly over and over to myself.

> 'I guess by the dear angel smile,
>   I guess by the love-rolling e'e,
> But why urge the tender confession
>   'Gainst Fortune's fell cruel decree, Jessie?'

I suppose I must have noted that his verses also commended a good many Jeans, several Peggies, one or two notable Marys, a Leslie, a Polly, even a Phyllis and a Chloris, without drawing the conclusion that the poet himself was something of a ranger, self-named Rantin' Rovin' Robin. It cannot be that I was ignorant of what I must call the Facts of Life: how could a country lad be unaware of them? It was simply that I did not apply them to humanity. It says little for the rare gift of a romantic heart that a man should come near to ruin for possessing one. Yet that was to be my fate.

A slip of once-white heather, now dried and brown, falls from the pages. We gathered it, young Jessie and I, in the late Autumn of 1870, which preceded the most bitter Winter in memory for our part of Scotland. From the first day of December the snow fell thickly, turning all Invermore into a sheet of white; white acres dotted with white trees, here and there the dark of an evergreen showing up, or the dirty cream fleece of a huddling sheep. Our shepherds tried in vain to fold them, for when the snow began the poor silly beasts had scattered in search of grass. Some had strayed as far away as Arrochar, some had wandered up the slopes of Inverbeg, to be found, bleached bones, when the Spring came.

The Castle shoots ceased. There were no house-parties, and Lord Invermore, in boots and oilskins, worked along with his tenants to rescue his animals. I mind well seeing an early-born lamb lying before our hearth, wrapped in Father's plaid, while Fiona held its limp head and Mother poured spoonfuls of warm milk between its soft jaws.

'We'll ha'e but a thin Yule,' Mother said to Father. 'I wonder how things are at Porthulish, Ian?'

Nothing had been heard from my Grandparents since the snow began, though it was their custom either to visit us or write a short letter every week. Grandmother knew well that Father worried about her, living in that lonely place, and part-crippled now with rheumatism. When he lectured her about the necessity for her to make Grandfather remove to a more civilised spot she would mock him in his own Lowland speech:

'Hush, ma babe, and dinna fret ye;
The Black Douglas shall na get ye!'

She could always annoy him with that jingle, the same she had sung to him in his cradle. And she refused to leave her home.

'When the day comes that I cannot put one foot before the other, I'll consider it,' she said; and that was the best Father could get out of her. As for Grandfather, he was impervious both to hints and straightforward suggestions, returning to both only his faint, humourless smile.

When three weeks had gone by and no word, Father determined on action. Somehow he would get through the snow to the road that led down beside Loch Long to Porthulish. It must be part-cleared by now, he reasoned, with traffic to and from Glasgow. Tired of inaction, I volunteered to go with him, against Mother's remonstrances.

Two bundles of clothing wearing wading boots, we set off a week before Christmas, with some provisions, along the path that had been cleared by the gardeners from the Castle gates to the small road beyond. Even as we drew almost out of sight of the gates the path became swiftly obscured by more snow. Father uttered one of his rare curses, but very softly, not to corrupt me.

We were three days on our journey, plodding stressfully for the best (or worst) part of it, sometimes almost buried under snowdrifts. Once we rested in the shelter of a covered haystack, and I, dog-tired, drifted into sleep, to be wakened by Father's shaking my shoulder frantically.

'Dinna nod off, Angus! The snow-sleep will finish ye!'

And every time my weary lids showed signs of closing he would rouse me by a shake or a prod. We were both bitterly cold and weary when a carrier picked us up on a stretch of the main road.

'How far to Porthulish?' Father asked him. We could scarce believe our numbed ears when the man said we were almost there. Familiar landmarks had been obliterated by the all-covering snow, the head of the wee river that straggled eastwards to Luss, the peak of Argyllshire across Loch Long. We might have been in Siberia, from what I had read of that place in the geography books.

It was about noon when we reached the first cottage of Porthulish. Thankfully we paid the carrier for conveying us, and all three of us entered the town's nearest inn. My Father did not even suggest that I should await outbye, firm as he had ever been that none of his children should go into such a place.

It was wonderfully warm, smoky and comforting inside. The landlady bustled out with cries of horror at our appearance, and hot toddy was pressed into our hands almost before we had time to fall thankfully on to a bench. There were few folk in the barparlour, for in such weather men stayed by their own firesides if they had any sense. One man was drinking with his back to us. He had a loaded pack on his shoulders, as though he was about to start on a journey. It was not until he finished his drink and turned to leave that I recognised Willie Allan. His face was ageless, perhaps because of his carefree life.

'Guid losh, man!' cried Willie to my Father. 'That I should meet you now! God send we're in time.' Seeing our startled faces, he said, 'Ye're bound for up yonder, are ye no'?' nodding towards the direction of the mountain.

'Aye, We've heard no' a word from them these three weeks.'

Willie's face was horrified. 'Ye've no' heard, then, that *he*'s awa'?'

Then he told us that he had returned the day before after two weeks down at Port Glasgow, where he had been working in the shipyard, to hear from the folk at the inn that my Grandfather had been there for his usual drinking-bout three weeks earlier. They knew nothing of where he went after such bouts, so that no questions were asked about how Grandmother was faring alone up on the mountain. Willie had been just about to set off to climb to the cottage when we entered the inn.

'Maybe he'll have gone straight hame,' I proffered hopefully.

'Aye, and maybe no',' snorted Willie. 'If he was back he'd be in here for a dram tae fortify him. We'd best set off while the licht's with us.'

It was a difficult, dangerous climb up the steep slopes, over icy boulders and sodden grass. The sheep-tracks had vanished. In some places the snow, exposed to the winds off Loch Long, had frozen stiff. I was not easy scared in those days, but I confess to fear then. As usual, the last lap was the longest.

At length we stood before the cottage. I think a chill colder than the snow fell on our hearts as we saw that no smoke came from the chimney. The windows were ice-covered; no hand had wiped them for days past.

In silence my Father tried the sneck of the door. It lifted, and the door gave to his touch. We went in.

The parlour was neat as ever, the table clear and the hearth swept. But the fire had gone out long before; the place was as chill as the grave. My Father went into the bedroom. I think Willie and I knew what he would find there, and we followed him with dread.

She was in her bed, the patchwork quilt she had made herself neatly laid over her. Her head was turned sideways on the pillow as if in peaceful sleep, her black silver-shot hair braided in two tidy plaits. Her face was terribly thin, emaciated as I had ever seen it, but a smile was on her lips. Across her feet lay her tabby cat Stuart, stiff and dead as she was.

My Grandmother had died of two causes: starvation and pride. Her proud heart would not let her go down the hill to the nearest cottage, half a mile away, to admit that her man had gone off on a mad cantrip, leaving her to face the winter days and nights, the dwindling supplies of food and fuel. Never should the world know that Robert Hudson had preferred a primitive bothy to the home his wife had made for him.

We discovered later that she had covered his absences over the years by telling neighbours that he was away visiting a sick sister, and his office that he was prone to a recurrent illness. If folk suspected, nothing was said. Only she and Willie knew his secret.

And so she had died peacefully, starved and half-frozen. Just as her ancestor Roderick did, she had sacrificed herself to save her prince; for a prince my strange Grandfather was to her, all their married life.

We carried her down the hill, wrapped in Father's plaid, and the three of us helped the sexton dig her a grave in the hard cold ground. A rough coffin was made for her, no bigger than a child's; the snow was falling on it as we lowered it into the grave in Port-hulish kirkyard. There were no flowers, no mourners, but Father, me and Willie, for she would not have wanted neighbours bidden.

'I am the Resurrection and the Life, saith the Lord: He that believeth me shall not perish.'

We shook hands with the Minister when the burial service had been said, and began our slow journey back to Garbeg.

CHAPTER FOUR

There is a gap of several months in my diary for 1871. I think it may be attributable to my age, for I was now in that difficult fifteenth year which is neither boyhood nor manhood, but something uneasy between the two. I remember that I was restless, wandering far afield by myself, away south down Glen Luss, or northwards to lovely Loch Sloy, lying like a blue jewel between the heights of Ben Vorlich and Ben Vane. I was much given to climbing the lower slopes of mountains, there to sit brooding, a wee speck in that grand landscape, pondering Life and Eternity.

Absorbed as I was in myself, I was not too mazed to notice the change in my Father. I think he was never the same man after the death of Grandmother. It was as though some power which had sustained him had departed, leaving him quieter, without his old merry laugh and hearty ways. Mother's face was marked with lines of worry, as she watched him stare blankly at a book without turning the pages, or jump out of his chair and stride irritably out of the house when Fiona and one of her friends were exchanging girls' gossip punctuated with daft giggles. Once he would have laughed at them, or bade them haud their whisht.

'D'ye think he's no' weel, Angus?' Donald whispered to me one night when Father had ordered us both to bed before our time, because we had disturbed his reading of the Bible with our clatter over a school-lesson.

I shook my head. 'It's in the mind. Fate's dealt him a sair blow.'

Two blows, to be accurate; for Grandfather had

never been seen since his final drink in Porthulish, in the previous December. When the Spring came, Father, Willie Allan and I went across the Firth to Arran, landing at Brodick, where we made our first enquiries; for Willie pointed out that it was a larger place than Corrie, and that Grandfather might well have come down from his eyrie to shelter there in the worst of the winter — might even have intended to take a boat back to the mainland, for his conscience must soon have told him to return to his wife.

But nobody at Brodick had seen a man corresponding to our description. We decided to walk to Corrie by way of wild Glen Rosa rather than by the coast road, in case Grandfather had found another mountain refuge there. A few huts we found, all deserted. As we neared Corrie and the spot where Willie had seen my Grandfather my heart beat rapidly, part in hope, but more in fear.

It was justified. The bothy was only a ruin, a few stones and rotting planks, the fire-place no longer bearing a trace of scorch-mark or ash. A heap of rabbit and pheasant bones were piled in the remains of the forsaken housestead. Father examined them, and the earth floor, from which he picked up a small object, and showed it silently to Willie.

It was a gold hoop earring.

'Aye,' said Willie. 'It would be hers, nae doot. Maybe he went off with her and the Romanies. But we'd best split up and search as wide as we can.' He sent me to the woods south of our situation, Father to the east, Willie himself taking a craggy western path, for he was as nimble as a mountain goat though no youngster.

It was sunset when we met again at the bothy; each trail had been unsuccessful. As we turned wearily down towards Corrie and the coast road, Father took the earring from his pocket and flung it in a great arc towards the dark trees, uttering as he did so the first strong oath I had ever heard on his lips.

I shall not forget my birthday in 1871. Here is my diary entry:

Today a great sorrow came to our house. One of the maids from the Castle called to say that a policeman from Glasgow was up there, speiring for Mrs. Hudson. Mother went with her alone, Father being out with the beaters. When Donald and I came in from the fishing we could see my Mother's face that there had been sore news. She was sitting at table, a cup of cold tea beside her.

'Angus,' she said, 'go and bring your Father from the moor. There's terrible tidings.'

I was afraid she would say Fiona had been hurt, for she had gone pony-riding that morning. It is strange how many visions of horror flash before the mind's eye at such a moment: I had seen our wee sister drowned, thrown from her beast's back, or caught in a spring-trap, before Mother spoke her next words.

'They hae found a man's skeleton on Arran. Twa fishers cam' on it by Machrie Water, in a lonely place. There was naething to say who it was but this.'

She laid on the table a many-bladed clasp knife, a common enough thing with a horn handle and blades long rusted. A silver plate had been let into the handle; I did not need to pick it up, for I had seen it often and knew what the name on that plate would be.

And so Grandfather came home to Porthulish at last, to lie beside the wife who waited for him; and Lord Invermore's piper played him to his burial.

The event which followed my last entry seemed at the time a calamity, but who are we to question Providence's ways? When Lord and Lady Invermore returned to the Castle after a stay in London, at the end of the game season, His Lordship sent for Father and told him that he had accepted the Governorship of Princess Amelia Island, a small British possession in the Gulf of Papua and British New Guinea.

'I know that this comes as a shock to you, Hudson,' he said.

'It does that, my lord,' said my Father.

'You will understand my motives better when I tell you that Lady Invermore's health has been causing me a great deal of anxiety of late. An eminent doctor examined her in London last week, and he has assured me that only a complete change of residence will benefit her. Warmth and freedom from the damp and cold of this climate are essential.'

'I ken Her Ladyship has a sair cough,' Father said. 'I wouldna like it if she were my wife.'

'Then you will understand,' said His Lordship, 'why I did not hesitate to accept the Prime Minister's offer of Princess Amelia Island, placed admirably for a person with her complaint.'

Father smiled inwardly, he told us, at His Lordship's innocent description; no doubt, good man, he thought the Island had been dropped in that particular area for the benefit of suffering Scots nobility. But he shook His Lordship's hand, and wished him luck and better health for his Lady.

'Naturally,' Lord Invermore went on, 'I shall see that neither you nor any of my people lose by our departure. The Castle will be let in our absence to friends of ours from England — Mr Edgar Rennishawe and his family. Mr Rennishawe will keep on all the staff, I understand, though he does not expect to occupy the Castle for many months at a time.'

It was a sad day when our Lord and Lady left us. A drizzle of rain turned the Castle and the grounds to a dull grey. We who stood alongside what was now known as the Queen's Drive were clad in our best blacks. Many of the women wept, including Mother and Fiona; some of the men, even, though I regret to say that their lachrymose condition was in part the result of the previous night's excesses. An honest lad, I confided to my diary that I was not guiltless in this respect.

My head was aching terribly with the whisky I had drunk at the Castle. Father was not for my going to the farewell feast, but His Lordship had particularly asked for me to be there, for it seemed I was something of a favourite of his. I fear I might like the drink too well if I was not canny about it. At first it warms the body and lights up the brain, turning even a sober lad like me into a wit. But then comes retribution, with a head full of stinging bees and a wambling wame. I was ashamed to think Her Ladyship might see me in such a state, but maybe she saw none of us clearly, with the tears running down her bonny face. Her colour was good, forbye, and I am glad she is away to a place where the sun shines.

'O Caledonia! stern and wild! meet nurse for a poetic child!' Thou art a cruel one to the frail in body. I thank God I was made strong.

As the carriage made its way to the gates some began to sing *Will ye no' come back again.* I was minded of Grandmother and Grandfather, and Roderick Mackenzie and the Prince, and I confess to you, dear diary, that I grat like a lass, and was not ashamed of it.

4 February, 1904

Shortly after reading those words written so long ago I was brought back to the present day by the chiming of St Peter's church clock. With some haste I made ready to superintend preparations for tonight's dinner-party, at which the guest of honour was to be Mr Arthur James Balfour, leader of the Conservative party and brilliant orator.

One of a butler's highest qualities is his ability to serve unobtrusively. To do this is a great pleasure to me, for I am a man to listen rather than to talk. To-night I enjoyed greatly the conversation at the table, covering as it did the vexed question of Home Rule for Ireland, the new trade policy. I noted with admiration that however controversial the topic, the gentle-men maintained the utmost politeness, never for one moment indulging in high words; and that the ladies, while maintaining an intelligent interest in the con-versation, contrived to remain on the fringe of it, exercising their social graces in contrast to the gentle-men's weightier contributions to the evening. (Though it troubles me slightly to see so much good food hardly tasted, when I remember my boyhood. How welcome to us was the sight of a plate of bannocks, or a bowl of porridge! How easily my poor Grandmother's life could have been saved by only one among those sump-tuous dishes — the Baron of Beef, the *saumon mousse*, the roast pork with oyster patties, the stuffed peaches in brandy. . . But these are reflections bordering on the Socialistic.)

What impressed me this evening, with the events recorded in my old diary so fresh in my mind, was the charm and grace of true aristocracy, in the person of Lady Marjorie and her circle. To the trained eye of a butler the distinction between the wheat and the chaff of Society is clear at a glance. I think I possessed it even as a youth, for at first sight I diagnosed the Rennishawes as chaff.

I turn back to my earlier diary.

15 December, 1871

The Rennishawe family arrived at the Castle today. In the afternoon they walked in the grounds to become acquainted with some of their tenantry, including our-selves.

I was home from the school when they arrived. Mr Edgar Rennishawe is a Member of Parliament. He is a tall, thin man with an eyeglass stuck in one eye. I cannot think how he keeps it there. His wife is particularly well-dressed but seemed out of temper. She was girning on to her husband about her boots being wet from the grass, and was slow to greet my parents. Me she did not address at all. They both spoke very fine English which we found sore to understand, and I saw Mother was blushing all over her face and neck, which is always a sign she is embarrassed.

Two of their sons were with them, one about my age called Harald, and an older one, Victor. It is said there is also a daughter away at school in Switzerland. I could not understand all they said, but thought their manner cold and most unlike that of His Lordship and Her Ladyship, who held us tenants as dear as their own family. When the Rennishawes had gone I saw that Father's face was set grim, and he whistled a tune as he took off his best coat and donned his old frieze jacket. I asked him what was the song. He gave me an unco queer smile.

> ' "For a' that, and a' that," ' he said,
> ' "Our toils obscure, and a' that,
> The rank is but the guinea's stamp,
> The man's the gowd for a' that." '

Boy as I was then, I sensed that something not welcome had entered our lives, as though a cold wind had begun to blow. Christmas and Hogmanay that year were shadows of what they had been in Lord Invermore's time. The customary presents of game and other delicacies were brought to the tenantry by the Castle servants and not by the family, as they aye had been; and if there was any merriment we saw nothing of it. Mr Victor and Mr Harald passed us without speaking in the grounds or on the moors. After one such encounter my Mother tossed her head and flushed with anger.

'I'm thinking English lairds are no' bred to respect

44

females,' she said. 'Yon Rennishawe lads could dae wi' some manners skelped into them.'

The Winter was long and dreary. After New Year came snow that laid until late in March. It was then I saw a change in my Father. Always in my memory upright and hearty, he had begun to stoop. He would ask one of us to help him pull off his boots nowadays, and I would often see him with a hand at the hollow of his back and his face creased with pain. At night he would take a steaming hot bath in the tin tub by the fire, and afterwards Mother would rub his back with liniment while he lay face downwards. One evening I heard him say to her in a voice not like his own:

'I'll need to tell him, Margaret.'

'Bide till the Spring, Ian!' she pleaded. 'Ye'll surely be better.'

But Spring came, and Father's aches and pains grew worse. Often it was I who went out to tend the young game-birds and scare off marauders, while he lay in his bed. It was in the fir-wood west of the Castle that I encountered Mr Rennishawe riding his bay mare. He reined her in at the sight of me and curtly beckoned me to him.

'Who are you and what the devil's your business here?' he asked.

I told him civilly enough that I was his keeper's eldest son. He seemed to accept this, though I could see he had no memory of my face.

'Why is your Father not at his work? I pay him enough besides his keep.'

'He's but poorly, sir,' I answered. 'He has the bone-ache from the bad Winter.'

Mr Rennishawe stared at me in his strange blank way for a moment. Then he said 'Send him to me at once!' and with a crack of the whip the mare was away.

I gave Father the message. When he returned from the Castle his lame step was at its slowest and his face

45

was grave. I was for leaving him alone with Mother, but he called me back. What he had to tell made cruel hearing. Mr Rennishawe had told him flatly that as he appeared incapable of work his services were no longer needed.

Mother's face turned white; I thought she was about to fall.

'But he canna!' she cried.

'He can that,' said Father. 'We're to be awa' by the weekend.'

Mother looked round the room like a woman dazed. 'But we'll lose oor hame!' she said, and fell into a fit of sobbing on Father's shoulder.

I left them alone, and went walking along my favourite path. The sun was beginning to set behind the young trees of Ardgarten Forest, on the yon side of Loch Long. Against the glowing sky the outlines of deer cropping the grass moved slowly, and on every side throstles and blackbirds poured out their songs. The old sheepdog Luath bounded out of a covert and ran ahead ahead of me barking after some fancied rabbit.

I thought of nothing. I have aye had a slow reflective mind, which takes long to debate and solve a problem. But somewhere in my boy's brain a still small voice sounded, telling me what I should do. I whistled up Luath, and with him beside me I set off briskly on the mile-long walk to Garbeg.

Through the front window of the Dominie's house I could see Mr Blair at his papers, working by the the sunset light. He looked up with surprise when his housekeeper showed me in.

'Why, Angus! Have ye not had enough lessons for today?'

His smile faded as he saw that I was not in the mood for cracking jokes, and he motioned me to sit down.

'Now,' he said, 'what news?'

46

Instead of telling him what had befallen us I burst out with a question.

'Sir, am I a good scholar?'

'Yes, indeed, Angus, though I could wish more speed to your pen.'

'Am I like to get the Greatheid Scholarship? Liker than Donald?'

Our Dominie mused. 'Well, that's hard to predict. You have the better all-round learning, but Donald has a special gift.'

I persisted in my inquisition. 'Would I make a better lawyer than Donald an architect?'

He looked at me thoughtfully from under his bushy brows. 'Only the Lord knows that, Angus. To my thinking you have a heart too soft for that way of life. Would you not consider teaching?'

I shook my head. 'I've always had a fancy for the Law. But sir, will you tell me fair and straight how I stand beside Donald in your judgment? I've need to know.'

Mr Blair laid down the quill whose feathers he had been smoothing, and sighed. 'I've no wish to damp your spirits, Angus, but since you ask I'll be plain with you. You're near sixteen, and a good steady scholar. There are many things you might do well in life. Donald is fourteen; and if I ever saw genius in my classroom, I see it in him. Yet in an academic contest you might well beat him.'

I rose. 'Thank you, Dominie,' I said. The good man watched me with surprise as I left his house and re-joined patient Luath.

When I reached home Father was sitting by the fire with Fiona on his knee; she had been greeting, and Mother's cheeks were wet. Donald had his books open on the table, but I knew that it had been long since he had turned a page. I felt I had left that room as a boy, and returned to it a man; and it was as a man that I spoke to Father.

47

'Dinna fret, for there's no cause. I'll be up to the Castle the morn and offer myself to Mr Rennishawe as gamekeeper.'

They stared at me like people turned to stone, and then all began to talk at once, telling me that I was clean daft and that the laird would never accept me. But when I presented myself before him the next morning, the five foot eleven of me kilted and plaided and as calm as a righteous soul before the Judgment Seat, within ten minutes I convinced that cold hard man that I was fit to take my Father's place, and that the cottage should remain our home.

Maybe I would have made a grand persuasive advocate, after all.

CHAPTER FIVE

Perhaps it is not surprising that there are no
further entries in my diary for more than a year. Every
moment of my time that was not spent in sleep was
given to work, harder work than I had ever known.
For I had to prove myself in a world where sleep
only comes briefly, and against men twice my age.

For I had not, of course, been appointed Head
Keeper in Father's place. There were other keepers
distributed about the length and breadth of the Invermore estate to whom I was but a babe in arms. Mr
Rennishawe acquired a great reputation throughout
the shire for his charity in letting the family of a
crippled keeper remain in the cottage, despite the fact
that the estate was unusually well provided with
cottages, and that several of the Invermore servants
lived in Garbeg itself. He knew full well that we Hud-
sons were good tenants, to be relied upon not to keep
cats or dogs that might turn wild among the game,
nor to filch eggs or birds for our own use. And when
I took Father's place our rent, which was taken from
my wages, was raised, so that I got only a few shillings
a week, which I gave to Mother.

But I cared nothing at all for Mr Rennishawe and
his penny-pinching. Because of me, Father could rest
his aching bones all day and afford a dram now and
then to ease the pain; and Donald, young as he was,
sat for the Greatheid Scholarship, and won it. In his
sixteenth year he became a student at Glasgow University, lodging with Auntie Ailie who lived there. It
was a proud day when we saw him off in the gig for
the station, flushed with happiness yet at the edge of
tears at leaving us. Our Dominie stood with us to see

him off. As the gig vanished from sight down the road he turned to me and laid a hand on my shoulder.

'Angus,' he said, 'There'll be a place kept for you in Heaven for what you've done for your Brother this day.'

I'm thinking that if I ever occupy that place it will not be for lack of earning it by the sweat of my brow.

At the earliest light of dawn I was always dressed and out, all seasons of the year, never coming home until the last of my work was done, and often rising again if a warning sound came to my ears. I had learnt keepers' lore since I was waist-high to Father, but now I had to use it or lose the laird's game and my place. It became second nature to me to search the ground for partridge-nests ill-placed where vermin could get at them. For the partridge nests on the ground, often near cover, and her enemies the stoats and weasels like cover to serve them as retreat when they have stolen eggs. My ears became sharp for the sound of uneasy chatter among the guinea-fowl, who sense the coming of stoat and fox; and for the flurry of movement among the bantams, huddling together when the fox was near.

The hardest part of all was the shooting of vermin. Yet they must be shot, to protect the game, and to stock the keeper's 'larder' which shows the laird that the labourer is worthy of his hire. My ash-pole gibbet was dutifully stocked with dead creatures, though not fully enough for the new Head Keeper, Archie McLeish. Every now and then he would arrive on a tour of inspection of the land in my keeping, and of my larder. The first time he saw that ugly gibbet his broad red face darkened.

'There's no' enough,' he said, pointing with his gun to the seven or eight limp bodies, rat, stoat and jay among them. 'Whaur's yer owls and yer hoodies, and sparrows, and a brock or twa?'

(I must say here, for the benefit of those who one

50

day may read these simple pages, that the badger's country name is Brock, and that hoodies or corbies are names for the common crow.)

I answered McLeish without fear; such men have no liking for weaklings.

'I let owls alane,' I said. 'They feed on rats and mice, that feed on the young birds and their eggs. Brock feeds on wasps, a nestfu' at a meal, and the hawk tak's sparrows in place of partridge chicks when they licht doon to the grain. It's live and let live wi' Nature, Mr McLeish.'

The keeper gave a wry grin. 'I see ye've got it a' worked out,' he said. 'Dinna let me hear of ony saftness, that's a'.' He moved on, his dog at heel. I knew that my way of thinking was right, for Nature has ordained that one beast should prey on another, and who are we to quarrel with her? If Man were to kill off rabbits, foxes would seek out farm animals; if sparrows became extinct, the hawk that pounces on the feeding-grounds would take the young game instead. The owl lives on mice and small creatures, just as the hedgehog and the toad keep the garden insects down. Each has its function. I should have been happier if my work had not dealt out death to any of God's creatures, even the snarling wild-cat who will bite the throat out of any beast or human threatening her blind kittens.

It troubled me, too, to go out with Mr Rennishawe and his party on a shoot, and to stand by as his loader, watching the birds I had tended all the year fall to the guns; one moment soaring against the sky, the next, limp bundles of bloody feathers across the jaws of retrievers. These days I found myself unwilling to eat game when it came to our table (which was less often than in Lord Invermore's time). Mother would shake her head and grumble that I was turning away good food, and I still growing, but even for her I

51

could not put knife into the flesh I had reared.

One enemy there was of everything on the estate for whom neither I nor any of the other keepers had any pity. Fences and gates have no terrors for the poacher; only the gun and the loaded stick put fear into his heart. We were fortunate in that Invermore lay in a peak of land between the two lochs, offering no invitation to travellers by road, and guarded by mountains. Yet the travelling tinkers and gipsy-folk slunk by night on the edges of the estate, hiding in copses and thickets, and when times were more than usual poor there would be city men coming from as far away as Glasgow to take what game they could get, by whatever means.

I am not a violent man — maybe it would have been better for me if I had been — but I confess I enjoyed pitting my strength as well as my wits against the vagabonds who came after our birds in and out of season, and who cared nothing for man or beast. I think that some of them poached for the sake of poaching, feeling that they were attacking the ruling class. Even in quiet little Garbeg the village politician, Johnnie Tyler, talked over his ale of Karl Marx and Friedrich Engels and their doctrine of Scientific Socialism. Mr Rennishawe was fair game to their followers, being an Englishman and a rich one, not the hereditary laird of Invermore.

I had many tangles with such men. My hearing was keen as a hawk's, my sense of smell so fine that I could all but smell poachers a field's length away (which was no wonder, for their scent was as rank as that of foxes.) More often than not the sight of me and my gun was enough to send them packing, but I remember with delight one occasion when I tried conclusions with one of the biggest rascals unhung. Though I only reached home when dawn was breaking, I got out my neglected diary and recorded my triumph.

Last night I came home early and tired. I slept soon, but woke just after midnight with the moonlight on my face. At first I thought this had caused me to wake, but after a moment I realised that for some reason I was not easy in my mind. I dressed and went out quietly, my feet taking me towards the spinney by the birch wood. The birds were quiet, only a hunting owl disturbing the night. As I approached the spinney a sudden scream told me that my instinct was right, that a poacher was out after hares.

In a thicket a dark form was moving among the shadows; by a beam of moonlight I saw the face. It was Irish Kevin, one of the road gang, the men who work by day on the new highway and prey on villages by night, taking what they can get. I was thankful for my fieldcraft that taught me to step so lightly, not even a twig cracking beneath my feet. I moved softly nearer to him, and perceived that he had two dead hares slung on his back and was about to take a live one which was struggling in a trap. And the trap was none of ours, that kill instantly by breaking the neck, but a home-rigged thing of wood and sharp wire in which a beast might stay living for a whole day and night, maiming itself by its efforts to be free.

Irish Kevin was so taken up with his work that he never saw or heard me until I stood beside him; then he straightened himself up with a black oath.

'I'll have those from ye, Irish,' I said, making to seize the dead hares. Without a word he began to use his fists on me, then, finding that he was making no headway got his hands round my throat. I wrenched them away, feeling murder in their clutch, and he fell backwards, taking me with him. I do not recall what happened next, but the struggle was a hard one, my youth and height against his solid brute strength. Nearby the guinea-fowl began their panicking chatter and unseen small creatures rustled away to safety, while the poacher and I rolled over and over, panting and cursing each other; I am glad the Minister was not by. At last, feeling that he was getting the worst of it, he struggled to his feet and ran off, towards the wood. Just as he reached it, while he was not yet in cover and the moonlight showed him plainly, I brought up my gun and peppered him in the legs. He gave a howl that must have roused the echoes as far off as Glen Douglas and staggered into the wood.

I let him go, knowing that I had done him no great harm but just enough to keep him from reaching the road. Then I bent down to the hare in the trap. It had been silent with fear as the poacher and I fought together, but now it began to scream at the touch of my hands. I untwisted the wire and freed him, taking him up to examine him for injuries. There were none yet. I felt his heart racing under my hand, then slowing as I stroked his soft fur in a way that told him he need fear nothing from me. Then I put him down and stood back. He was still for a minute, gathering his wits, then louped off in great strong bounds of his back legs.

Maybe he will die in the next hare drive, or in another trap. But though I shall not confess it to any of the other men who would think me a fool, I was as glad to have freed him as to have routed Irish Kevin.

This morning we found Irish on the further edge of the birch wood, unable to stand or sit and groaning fearfully. He is now in the hands of the police.

As I read that boyish boast, made thirty-one years ago, I cannot quite believe that I am a man of forty-eight and that this is the year 1904. I still smell the freshness of that June morn, when I led Mr McLeish to the wounded poacher. It is, alas, all too true that in a man's middle age he recalls old times far more vividly than recent events. For the past two months I have been in Scotland with Mr Bellamy, acting as his valet and as loader during shoots. Every year, for the past twenty or so, I have done this, the weather and the company varying from year to year, all else the same. I can barely remember the faces of the gentlemen staying at our shooting-lodge in Perthshire, distinguished though many of them were. On our return to London I learnt that Sarah Moffat had left the household after a disgraceful frolic in which she and other servants took advantage of the family's absence; and, although I recall her as a handsome girl of a rather bold type, I cannot summon up her features in my mind.

Perhaps the head grows old, but not the heart. I mind the words of Robert Louis Stevenson, written to an old Jacobite tune.

'Sing me a song of a lad that is gone;
   Say, could that lad be I?
Merry of soul he sailed on a day
   Over the sea to Skye.'

The lad that was I stands at my side, as I look back to Christmas 1874, when Miss Adela came home.

*   *   *   *

In all the time since I had been a keeper I had seen little of the Rennishawe family. Much of their time was spent in London, or at their home in County Durham, though it was said that this had become less agreeable to them with the growth of Tyneside industry. Mr Victor and Mr Harald took little interest in the estate and its affairs, spending most of their leisure time during the late summer months playing tennis on the court they had laid out with Lord Invermore's permission, and appearing not to recognise such small fry as gamekeepers or gardeners. Mr Rennishawe, like his sons, had what Mother described as a gey cauld eye, though he took some part in the working of the estate and usually accompanied his bailiff on tours of inspection; while Mrs Rennishawe was something of an invalid, suffering from migraine headaches. We hardly knew her by sight.

In general I kept away from the Castle itself, conscious that tenants were not welcome in its vicinity. But it happened that a day or two before Christmas I was out early training a pup of Luath's, a fine gundog in the making.

He stayed at heel for some while, but suddenly, as pups will, he dashed off barking wildly at some imaginary object. I whistled him back, and he came fawning and wagging his whole body, only to dart off again out of sight. I pursued him almost to the Castle stables, then lost him. I paused to scan the distance for him, when round the corner came a horse and rider. It was one of the greys, a high-stepping mare, ridden by a young lady I had not seen before.

She drew rein and stopped smartly, addressing me in a loud clear English voice.

'You'd be well advised to take better care of your dog, my man! He nearly had the mare down.'

The pup had returned and was dancing round the mare's hooves. The rider shouted a command at him, at which he instantly lay flat, looking up at her out of the corners of his eyes.

I made some apology, conscious that I was blushing and angry with myself for it. She studied me curiously, then leapt down from the mare; I saw her clearly then, and I see her now. She was tall for a girl, slender enough to carry off the wasp-waisted figure of the time without seeming tortured by it. Her dress was dark green, the colour of ivy leaves, her cloak black; a hood over her hair, the colour of pale moonlight (I was proud of myself for that fine phrase). As for her face, I could hardly describe it, except that it was without the touch of paint I had seen the ladies of the Castle wear. But she was unmistakably a Rennishawe; Mr Victor and Mr Harald were in her looks, as well as the laird himself.

She stared at me as intently as I at her, before she asked:

'What's your name, young man?'

I told her, feeling strangely ashamed of it. She laughed mockingly.

'Hudson! I thought all you Scotsmen were called Mac This That and T'other.'

'My Father's folk came from Glasgow,' I said.

'Ma Faither's folk cam' frae Glesca'!' She parroted my accent, making me flush more deeply and wish I were anywhere else. 'And whaur's yer hame, Angus Hudson?'

I waved vaguely towards the direction of our cottage, giving her some even vaguer directions, and furious with myself for my clumsiness. She nodded.

'I'll pay you a social call one of these days,' she said. 'How would you like that, Angus Hudson?'

I stammered that it would be a great honour, and was going havering on about my Father's illness when she interrupted me.

'I'm Adela Rennishawe. I'm home for good from that bloody school and I'm never going back.'

Shock at hearing such a word from a lady's lips kept me silent. My face evidently amused her. She remounted the mare and looked down at me with a wicked smile.

'Why d'you think I stopped to talk with you?'

I shook my head dumbly.

'Because,' she said, 'I like a lang lad richt weel. Who said that, Angus Hudson?'

If she had asked me who wrote the Old Testament I could not have been more nonplussed.

'Mary, Queen of Scots! Will you be my Darnley, Angus Hudson?' She struck the mare a crack with her whip and cantered off, out of sight, leaving me a prey to confused feelings in which anger, shame, and

57

excitement predominated. I wandered away, the pup now obedient at my heels, cooling my red face in the frosty air and trying to marshal my thoughts.

I spoke to no one of my encounter. But in my diary for that day a single sentence is written:

'Miss Adela Rennishawe spoke to me.'

CHAPTER SIX

Even today I feel a real pain somewhere beneath the second button of my waistcoat as I look at the record of those days. It varies from the brief to the rhapsodic, and from the rhapsodic to the clean daft.

I saw Miss Adela return from driving. She seemed not to see me. How can I have offended her?

Miss Adela out with the guns. She admired Tam (Luath's pup) saying he was a fine dog.

A house-party at the Castle. Waited in the gardens to hear the dance-music from the ballroom, knowing SHE was dancing there. Saw HER come out on to the balcony with a gentleman. She had a glass in her hand and was laughing. She wore a gown of yellow like a daffodil. O my princess, my queen, my Adela! When wilt thou see that an honest manly heart is worth more than the flattery of Lords? When wilt thou bend down from thy steed to give him thy fair hand, who dared not touch even thy boot?

Even to my own infatuated eye this last appeared the least bit ridiculous. Dissatisfied with my prose, I broke into verse.

> 'There lives a lass in yonder Ha'
> And fair is she abune them a',
> Wha keeps my heart in unco' thra' . . .'

I was not, evidently, a budding Rabbie Burns. Truth to tell, I hardly knew what, or who, I was. To a modern young man it would seem laughable that at the age of eighteen I had never been in love, apart

59

from my childish fancy for Jessie Lukar, had hardly given it even a thought; that I knew nothing of women beyond my Mother, Fiona, and Fiona's friends from the school, who seemed to me no more than children. I was, in fact, a complete innocent, unable to reason out the state of my own feelings. I had, hardly realising the process, become a man, at the sight of a comely woman, even as Adam knew not his own nature until the Lord gave him Eve.

Those about me could not fail to see that something ailed me. Mother scolded me for my new untidiness, for clothes left in the middle of the floor because I had gone into a dream while doffing them. Mr McLeish sent for me to deliver a harangue because I had omitted to move a partridge's nest from a bad position, in consequence of which a weasel had got the eggs and killed the hen-bird. He called me a doited young noddie, and prophesied that I would shoot myself with my own gun if I continued in my shiftless ways.

Often I brooded darkly on the thought of inflicting on myself just such an end. Would Miss Adela weep, I wondered, when my bleeding corpse was carried past her? Would Mr Rennishawe insist on my lying in state in the Castle hall, two junior keepers at my head and two at my feet, my dead face serene in the light of four tapers? It seemed improbable, but such musings relieved my feelings, so often wounded by Miss Adela's coldness or by her deliberate taunting of me. It amused her to saunter up to me in the hearing of others and mock me with the cruel imitation of my voice, or to change course suddenly and go by me without speaking, her head haughtily tilted. My blushes and broodings became a joke on the estate. Only wee' Fiona seemed to understand and pity me. At fourteen she had all a woman's intuition. Watching my anguished gaze towards the Castle, she said with gentle wonder:

'What for do ye like her, Angus? She's no' even bonnie.'

Fiona was right. Miss Adela was no beauty. Her nose was inclined to the snub, her brow unbecomingly high, her eyes a cold grey. Her hands were large and bony, her figure too flat. When she was old she would look like Queen Elizabeth of England, for all that she saw herself as a passion-inspiring Mary Stuart. I knew all this, but my feelings were unchanged.

It was in the Spring, when our woods awoke to green loveliness, and all Nature seemed in a rapture, that my cold goddess began to relent. One day as I sat by the loch, hoping for a fat carp or two to rise to my line, a rustling in the grass behind me made me turn my head.

She stood there, tall as a lad in her long plaid skirt, a shawl round her shoulders like a peasant lass. On her face was the mocking grin I feared to see, but she spoke pleasantly enough.

'Have you caught anything?'

'No, Miss Adela.'

'May I join you? Or will I frighten the fish?'

I stammered my willingness, and she plumped down beside me and for some minutes conversed as freely as with any gentleman of her own class. My shyness left me, and I became quite loquacious. Suddenly she rose.

'I must go back. Will you ride with me tomorrow? Early, about seven?'

I could barely get out a reply for the emotion that choked me. When she was out of sight I laid by my rod and fished out my current diary, dog-eared from many sojourns in my pocket, and began to compose an ode in which Adela became Anna, the Flower of Invermore, and I her swain. There are not many romantic-sounding rhymes to Adela.

I hardly slept that night. At dawn I was up, listening impatiently to my Father's snores, inspecting my face keenly in my bit of mirror to see had the hateful spots left it, smoothing my hair down with a wet comb. At the first touch of sun I was out and away.

I had chosen my horse, a quiet chestnut, from the stable (I dared not risk a sprightly beast) when she appeared. She wore her tartan rig again, and looked as smiling as the day before. I was in Paradise, riding at her side, hearing from her gossip about the Castle, about English society and other matters I barely comprehended. Before I knew it we were entering the same birch wood where I had caught the poacher.

'I wish to walk,' she said imperiously.

I dismounted and gave her my hand, and she alighted. She held it in hers, leaving her horse to wander free. I felt acutely conscious of her closeness, feeling that in some way it was presumptuous of me to let her hold my hand. I was about to free it under the pretext of knotting my own mount's reins, which were trailing loose, when she turned to face me, our bodies touching and our eyes almost on a level.

If her holding of my hand had been embarrassing, this was even worse. Was she, I wondered, going to ask me to extract something from her eye? But her gaze was unclouded and direct, even sharp.

'Ah, well,' I said nervously, 'Maybe we should move on.'

'Ahweel,' she mocked me, 'mebbe we shouldna. Are you going to kiss me or not, Angus Hudson?'

Kiss her? I recoiled, shocked. What I had expected of this morning ride I knew not, but it was certainly nothing to do with kissing; a communion of souls, perhaps, or a knightly declaration of vows on my part and a sweet acceptance on hers. I knew my place far too well for anything more daring. Besides, we were not much of a family for kissing, and I had never practised it apart from a fond peck at my Mother's cheek on her birthday or the New Year.

But something in Miss Adela's gaze told me that

she might become exceedingly angry with me if I refused her strange request. Awkwardly I touched her cheek with my lips and then jumped back as though the cheek had been on fire instead of freshly cold. She looked at me like a woman torn between disbelief and fury.

'*Well!*' she said, and the sound was like the explosion of a gun. 'If that's all you're good for, Angus Hudson, you can continue the ride by yourself, and damn you to hell!' Before I could speak she was on her horse and galloping off the way we had come.

To say that I was shocked by this episode would be an understatement. My innocence had been rudely shattered, together with my image of Miss Adela as a kind of goodness. And yet she had aroused feelings in me which kept me awake at night, and made me something other than and less than myself. I was ashamed of her and of my thoughts; feared to meet her, yet hung about places in which she might be.

She let me simmer for a week. Then, one day in April, a day of gentle rain, she and I met late in the afternoon, as I made my way to the rearing field. That night I made one of my now rare entries in my diary.

14 April
Miss A. has forgiven me. We walked together for an hour and she was sweet as honey. The other was all my fancy. I tried to ask her to pardon me for my thoughts about her, but could find no words. We parted friends: I hope we shall remain so.

Alas for my hopes. Several times these encounters took place, never by my contriving, and always they left me uneasy. If it were not unkind to her, I would have wished her back in London or at Aycliffe Hall. And yet a part of me longed for her.

There came an evening when I wandered out by the sunset light, my mind on nothing more than a pair of rogue dogs that were rumoured to be after our bantams. I inspected the farm fences, finding no gaps, and bade goodnight to Dougal who cared for the fowls, on his way to the inn at Garbeg. Seeing the barn door swinging loose I looked in, to make sure no stray animal had entered.

She was there. If I live to my century I never shall forget seeing her, hands on her hips and that hateful, beckoning smile on her face, waiting for me. I knew, without telling, that she had seen me on my rounds and guessed what my actions would be; that she had opened the barn door and laid a trap for me. And yet I could not help but move towards her, as if she pulled me by a magnet. Still I did not speak or touch her, until she suddenly put her hands to her head, and scattering pins in all directions pulled down her hair. It lay about her shoulders, down as far as her waist, that milky hair. I had never seen a wicked fairy, but I knew their likeness then.

'Angus,' she whispered, 'handsome Angus.'

'By, but you're bonnie,' I said; and before I knew it we were lying on a pile of hay in the corner of the barn.

Even now I shudder to think of the events that followed. At one moment we lay there clasped, a dove cooing somewhere up in the roof, a few stray hens pecking about the floor, and I was learning what kissing meant to Miss Adela; the next moment the barn door had flown open and Mr Rennishawe was there, looking down at us. He was in riding-gear and carried a riding-crop.

I scrambled up and began to stammer something, but Miss Adela anticipated me. She began to shriek and moan, and I saw that her blouse was torn at the shoulder, not by my hands.

'Oh, Papa!' she cried. 'Oh, thank God you came in time! I've been so frightened — he was too strong for me — in another minute it would have been too late! Oh, take me away, please!'

She ran to him and buried her face against his coat. His expression did not change, but, pushing her aside, he advanced on me and cracked the riding-crop about my shoulders.

'Get out,' he said.

I lost no time in doing so.

* * * *

20 April, 1875

Tonight I drained the cup of disillusion. The iron entered my soul. I have done with women.

I smile as I read that bitter entry. Little did I know — but that lay far ahead in time.

Every day, after the episode in the barn, I lived in fear of Mr Rennishawe sending for me to give me the formal dismissal that would take the bread out of my family's mouth and the roof from over their heads. My Father helpless, my Mother ageing, Fiona still at school, and Donald away in Glasgow costing more than his scholarship grant would cover, myself turned off without a character, work in our part of Scotland as scarce as hens' teeth: it was a prospect to appal. Or would the laird choose to call on us in person, rapping on the cottage door with the butt end of that crop which had struck me so painfully? Would there, alternatively, be a brief note brought by a smirking servant from the Castle?

In the event none of these things happened. It appeared that Mr Rennishawe had decided to ignore the whole matter. Gradually I ceased to tremble with apprehension whenever I heard footsteps approaching me, at home or in the fields. One day Mother mentioned that the Rennishawes and Miss Adela had been seen driving to the station, and that Elspeth from the Castle had heard that they were going abroad for the summer. I drew a breath of relief which caused Mother to look at me in a very old-fashioned manner. I knew then that she and Fiona had had a wee bit clack about the grand young lady who was no' bonnie, and their daft young Angus.

Strange to say, the forbearance of Mr Rennishawe increased my respect for him, for I sensed that it betokened no weakness on his part, but the fact that he knew his daughter and her nature, and declined to use me as a scapegoat for her misdemeanour. My opinion was confirmed by an opinion of her expressed by Dougal at the farm, in a remark which I will not repeat, but which concerned the aptness of her milky hair to her inclinations.

I shall never forget Miss Adela; her uncanny charms, her effect on my life, and, most of all, her treachery. It is the grandest cure for love I know.

Here, in my diary for late 1875, are some scribblings of poor verse, a piece of gamekeepers' lore given to me by Mr McLeish, a recipe for liniment from Mr Blair's housekeeper, considered infallible for rheumatism. For my Father's illness was the thing uppermost in my mind in those days. Though not yet forty-five he was as bent as an old man, his face drawn into lines of pain and his joints gnarled like the boughs of trees. Mother had made him up a bed in the parlour, since he could no longer climb the stairs. She now shared the bedroom with Fiona, and I slept in a turn-up bedstead near Father; not that I could get much sleep for his turning and groaning.

I recall him saying to my Mother one day, as he watched her bustling about, working to keep our small home swept and polished:

'I'm a sair trouble to ye, Margaret.'

She turned a smiling face to him. 'Ye're no trouble at all, ye ken that fine. The day I canna work, they

66

can carry me oot, feet first.' Her hand flew to her mouth as she realised what she had said; but Father did not reproach her. They both knew how unlikely it was that he would ever leave the cottage on foot again, or walk with his dog and gun in the rearing-field and on the moor. He had aye been a brown man, the tan of his face all the darker for his fair hair. Now both were as grey as any miner's. He looked down at his misshapen hands, twisting with inactivity.

'I try no' to repine,' he said. 'The guid Lord sends these things to test our spirits. I hae tried to pass the time reading His Word, but the Buik's gey heavy.' And so it was, our great black-backed Family Bible with the brass clasps and all our names and birth-dates inscribed within the cover. Mr poor Father's crippled hands and feeble strength were scarce enough to hold it. I had made him a reading-stand to keep by his bed, but he had to sit up in a twisted posture to read from it, and it was not often he got beyond half a chapter of the Scriptures.

He liked best for Mother or Fiona to read to him, when all was quiet in the evening, a pup of Luath's line asleep on his knees, the lamp-wick turned up to throw a bright light on the page. I read nothing today that brings tears to my eyes like the memory of a woman's gentle voice reading aloud the opening canto of *The Lay of the Last Minstrel*:

> 'The way was long, the wind was cold,
> The Minstrel was infirm and old:
> His wither'd cheek and tresses gray
> Seem'd to have known a better day;
> The harp, his sole remaining joy,
> Was carried by an orphan boy.
> The last of all the Bards was he,
> Who sung of Border chivalry;
> For, welladay! their date was fled,
> His tuneful brethren all were dead,

And he, neglected and oppress'd,
Wish'd to be with them, and at rest.'

Often it happened that by this time Father's eyelids had dropped, lulled by the verse, and Mother
would softly close the book. Then the heavy eyelids
would lift.
'Go on, Margaret.'
'I thocht ye were asleep.'
A smiling shake of the head would answer her, and
she would continue.

'The Duchess mark'd his weary pace,
His timid mien, and reverend face,
And bade her page the menials tell
That they should treat the old man well;
For she had known adversity,
Though born in such a high degree;
In pride of power, in beauty's bloom,
Had wept o'er Monmouth's bloody tomb.'

Sometimes, when the reading was finished, but
Father still in too much pain to sleep, we would all
talk, as I flatter myself only Scots folk can talk, of
our country's history, so bound up with our lives; of
that same Monmouth grovelling in silk bonds before
his remorseless Uncle, King James, who threw away the
throne; of King James's son, the King Over the Water;
and his Grandson, the White Rose Prince who shone
upon Scotland like the morning star in the year of '45,
and who left her a ruin.
Then, at last, Father would sleep, and we could
creep away.
I see a diary entry for this time, after one such
evening.

They call the Nine of Diamonds the Curse of Scotland. It may have been so for the Royal Stuarts; for

us commoners I am sure the Curse of Scotland is the rheumatism that comes from our climate, our mists and rain, to bend our backs while we are yet young.

At that point I laid down my old diary to prepare myself for supper. I was back in the present year, 1906, and yet my mind lingered in that quiet scene of long ago, contrasting it with our gathering in the servants' hall tonight.

Lady Marjorie and Mr Bellamy were out for dinner, Miss Elizabeth staying in Bordeaux with friends, to tutor their children in the English language and incidentally to recover from the symptoms of depression following her unhappy infatuation with the so-called Baron Klaus von Rimmer.

She had certainly behaved foolishly in that affair, but I cannot help feeling sympathy for her in the cruel disillusionment she had suffered. I know too well the pain such an experience can cause. Thank Heaven the scandal is no longer discussed in our household, and even the fall of the Conservative Government has ceased to cause gloom; we are, in fact, back to normal.

After the meal, at which I had to reprove Edward for reading a betting journal propped up against the milk-jug, we settled down in our different ways. Emily was washing up, smashing only the occasional cup or saucer, before repairing to Brompton Oratory to make her confession. Rose was mending some garment for Miss Elizabeth, while Mrs Bridges sat at the table studying her Dream Book.

' "Cats, Black," ' she read out. ' "Do not expect good fortune from this dream. It signifies that you have a secret enemy." '

'Must be the butcher's boy,' Rose suggested. 'Twice he's brought Lady Knaresborough's order instead of ours.'

'That's right,' said Mrs Bridges. 'Nearly put my luncheon arrangements out, and laughed in my face when I told him off. Not much secret about him, cheeky young devil.'

Rose was sighing over her needlework. 'I don't half wish Sarah hadn't gone off like that. Sewing comes natural to her, not like me. Look at this dratted flounce, down again, where Miss Lizzy's caught her heel.'

'And where might you be going?' I enquired of Edward, who was getting his coat from the row of pegs.

'Down to the pub for a pint,' he replied. 'That's unless I'm wanted.'

I gave him a nod of approval, but Miss Roberts, who never misses an opportunity to disapprove, sniffed loudly and muttered something about iniquity and corruption, provoking Edward into a musical invitation to 'Come, Come, Come and 'ave a drink with me, Dahn at the Old Bull and Bush'. I gestured to Edward to leave before an unseemly brawl could develop.

' "Child," ' said Mrs Bridges, turning over another page of her Dream Book. ' "To dream of a child is unlucky and may portend disaster." Oh dear! Only last night I dreamed. . .' she flushed painfully and became silent.

Emily appeared at the door wearing her hat and coat, which was sufficiently open to reveal that she had on her rosary.

'May I go out, please, Mr Hudson?' she asked timidly. I intimated that she might. As the door closed behind her Miss Roberts addressed me.

'How you can encourage such Heathen practices, Mr Hudson, you with your good Protestant upbringing, I'm sure I cannot imagine.'

'And who may you be to criticise other people's religions, might I ask?' enquired Mrs Bridges, bridling. 'I suppose you call my Dream Book Heathen practices, too?'

'Of course.'

'Well, I don't see *you* reading anything but *Hilda's Home Companion*,' Mrs Bridges snapped. I saw the usual bickering match beginning, and smiled to myself as I wondered what would be the result if I began a discussion about the rival claims of Elizabeth Tudor and Mary Stuart to the throne of England. I fear that the English have lost the art of conversation — that is, if they ever had it. The fire was warm on my face. I let the daily newspaper subside on my chest, and drifted back into that little parlour of long ago, where my poor Father too was falling asleep, my Mother silently preparing for bed, and Fiona's dark head drooping over *Marmion*.

CHAPTER SEVEN

In the Spring of 1876 sad news came to us from abroad. Lady Invermore was dead. The balmy air of Princess Amelia Island had not cured her complaint, and by the time we heard of her death she had been buried far from the Scotland she loved.

All hoped that Lord Invermore would return, since the island must have painful memories for him; but week after week passed by with no intimation of this. The Rennishawes were generally disliked by all our people for the distance they kept between themselves and us, and for other traits. Mr Rennishawe was thought niggardly in his management of the estate through his English bailiff, his sons had a name for high-handedness and cruelty, while Mrs Rennishawe barely showed her face outside the Castle. Miss Adela was not seen, and it was rumoured that she was to be married in England.

It was a surprise to us all when a maid from the Castle appeared at our door with a letter addressed to Mother and bearing the Rennishawe crest. Mother read it slowly. When she looked up from it her eyes were round with surprise.

'Why, here's Mistress Rennishawe wanting our Fiona to wait on her!' she exclaimed. 'Wonders'll never cease.'

It proved that Mother's friend Elspeth had been consulted by Mrs Rennishawe, who wanted a clean and capable young girl to attend on her as lady's maid, her own having left. She had recommended Fiona, now fifteen, a well-grown lass, not the brightest of Mr Blair's scholars but with a wonderfully neat hand for domestic work. At first my parents were loath to let her go, and I myself had taken a scunner against the folk at the Castle since my unfortunate experience with Miss Adela, for all that I had a certain respect for the laird for sparing me punishment. Father decided Fiona's fate; from his couch he saw more than those of us who had the use of our limbs.

'It'll mak' or break the lassie. Gin she learns nae mair she'll learn something of the warld's ways.'

Indeed she did, as I recorded in my diary.

11 May, 1876

Fiona home for the first time. She has grown a full inch and filled out with the Castle's fare, which she says is grand. Nothing spared, game and salmon, sweet cakes that the English love, and a sweet warm drink called chocolate. Mrs Rennishawe does little but lie on a sofy reading novels from Mr Kelso's library or from Kilmarnock, while Fiona dresses her hair with pins and puffs of horsehair. She and Mr Rennishawe speak together very little. When they dine they take opposite ends of the table and Mrs Rennishawe continues to read.

Mr Victor and Mr Harald are expected next month. Mr Harald has a new wife, a Frenchwoman, they say.

2 June

Father is much worse today. When I came home in high feather, having at last shot the sparrowhawk that was harassing our chicks, I found him in great pain, and Doctor Jamieson sent for. The Doctor was scarcely gone when we received a surprise visit from Mr Rennishawe, the first he has paid us this year. It seems he saw the Doctor's gig driving away and wondered who was ill. He looked very sour at Father, and did not smile when Father in his pain cracked a wee joke, saying that the bone-ache had worn itself oot killing Rabbie Burns, and hadna the strength left to do for *him*. Mother asked the laird how Fiona was proving, and he replied sharply that she was giving satisfaction, so far as he knew.

As Mr Rennishawe went away I saw him talking with the bailiff, their heads very close.

Two days later I see an entry in almost an unrecognisable handwriting; but I know it is my own, dashed down in wild fury.

5 June

I scarcely know how to write this. Today Fiona came running to me in the rearing-field, crying 'Angus, come! Angus, he's taken Brown Bobby. . .'

I am back again, the sun hot on my head, pheasants whirring their displeasure at the noise my sister was making as she wept against my shoulder, her hair streaming loose, her voice hoarse with tears. I stroked her as if she had been a frightened horse, until she could gasp out her story. Brown Bobby was a retriever who had been Lord Invermore's favourite, a beautiful creature the colour of beech leaves in Autumn. He had a gentle spirit and the softest mouth for game any dog ever owned: if a partridge chick strayed near danger Bobby would bring it back as softly as though it had been a puppy, and lay it unharmed at my feet. There was no dog to match him at Invermore, not even the progeny of our dead Luath.

When she was calm enough, Fiona managed to tell me that she had been spending an hour free from her duties in the field where the blackfaced Highland sheep graze, high up and looking across the loch to Ben Lomond. Bobby had gone with her, as he often did; he was sitting quietly by the stile on which she was perched when hoofbeats came drumming towards them, and Mr Victor Rennishawe appeared, riding his black horse. As he approached the fence he set the horse to jump it, shouting to Fiona to get out of the way. She leapt off the stile just in time to avoid being hit by the flying hooves, and fell to the ground, while Bobby rushed off in pursuit of the horse and sheep scattered in all directions from beneath the trees where they were resting.

Mr Victor shouted and swore at the dog, which took no heed of him. Before Fiona could pick herself up he was unhorsed, sprawling on the grass, with Bobby barking and dancing around him.

'And then, Angus, he got up and dragged Bobby by the collar and went off toward Stuckgowran wood, with a stick hooked in Bobby's collar, and I ken fine he'll no' bring him back alive!'

'Whisht, lassie, whisht,' I said. 'I'll do what I can.' And I ran with all the power of my long legs towards Stuckgowran. As I neared it I could see the green check jacket of the Englishman moving against the trees, and my heart sank for fear of what I would find.

He heard my approach, and turned to face me with a sneering smile. From the low-growing bough of an oak-tree something brown swayed to and fro. A limp feathery tail almost brushed the ground. I looked upwards to the rope that creaked with the weight of the dog's corpse.

As I have remarked before, I am not a man of violent passions. I do not expend emotion on trivial things, and I have therefore all the more to spare when anger takes hold of me, as it did then. I put my two hands round Victor Rennishawe's neck and shook him as a terrier shakes a rat, until his grinning English teeth chattered, while his hands scrabbled at mine. Then I deliberately loosed my hold so that he would be free to attack me. To the feeble battery of his fists I replied with the heaviest blows my own hard fists could deal, knocking the wind from his lungs and the balance from his legs, while he choked and spluttered and I kept up a running fire of talk, half-mad as I was.

'Could ye no' have shot him?' I asked, landing a

well-directed right on his jaw, and rejoicing to feel some teeth loosen and see a trickle of blood from the corner of his mouth. 'Could ye no' have dealt fairly wi' a dog that was guarding your ain lambing ewes?' I struck him a body-blow over the heart, and he collapsed on the ground, groaning but still conscious. I gave him a contemptuous kick. Then I cut the rope and lowered what had been Bobby, holding it in my arms like a bairn. He had died quickly, thank the Lord, and not by slow strangulation: his neck was broken. I laid him in the shade beneath a bush of wild-roses, until I could return and bury him.

Then, bloody and grimed that I was, I marched up to the Castle and rang the bell. The English butler who answered the door told me that his master was engaged. I pushed him aside and went in.

There was a sound of voices from a room which I knew to be the library. I walked in without knocking, the butler protesting behind me. Four men were sitting in armchairs; there was a haze of pipe-smoke in the room. On a table at Mr Rennishawe's side was a silver tray holding a whisky decanter. I went up to him, shaking off the butler who was plucking at my sleeve and saying that he had tried to stop me entering. All the company stared at me as though I had been a fearsome kelpie from the depths of the loch; and indeed I must have looked not unlike one.

'Mr Rennishawe,' I said, 'I have just given your son Victor the sairest beating he'll get this side the tomb, and I'm here to tell ye the truth of it.'

'Kind of you,' he said with a cold smile. 'Continue, pray.'

'Today your son murdered the grandest dog that ever followed the guns of Invermore, and his Lordship's favourite forbye, for no worse a crime than daeing its duty.' And I told them of Fiona's frightening, and of the hanging of Brown Bobby. 'Now, I concluded, 'ye ken the facts. Thanks to your son's prank there's a ewe dropped her lamb before time, and maybe ithers will follow; and a dog that's brocht ye mony a pheasant has suffered a felon's death. I trust his hangman'll no' get off scot-free.'

For all my heat I was aware of my listeners' surprise and shock. Mr Rennishawe had allowed his cigar to burn itself out in the marble ashtray at his side. His face had a pale ugly look to it.

'You've quite finished ranting?' he enquired.

'Aye, sir.'

'Then take your filthy boots off my hearthrug and yourself out of my house.'

His angry eyes met mine.

'Ye tellt me that before,' I said. 'Your son's a butcher and your daughter's a hoor. I wish ye joy of them.' I did not care what I said. There was a red mist of rage dancing before my eyes, blending with the summer sunshine, veiling the Englishmen in their costly tweeds and the golden whisky in the square cut-glass decanter. I felt as though half a pint of Auld Glenlivet were inside me; as if I could fight a dozen men with one hand tied behind my back. Somewhere in the mist a voice was saying 'You'll regret, this, Hudson', and an anxious hand was pulling at my sleeve, urging me towards the door. It was the butler, all a-tremble with fear of his own dismissal. I let him lead me out of the room. My last glimpse of it surprised me, for it was a smile on the face of one of the guests: a kindly smile, I thought with wonder.

I stayed out late that night, after I had buried Bobby under the rose-tree. I took off his collar with its silver plate engraved with his name, for I thought Lord Invermore would be glad to have it. Then I walked, not caring where I went, along the shores of Loch Lomond and westwards through Glen Douglas, towards the setting sun. It was in my mind to go into Garbeg and drink myself mindless at the inn. Then I thought that I would be needing every penny in my pocket soon, for I had brought ruin on myself and my family. But if I had my time over again, Bobby, I said to the brown ghost walking beside me, its gentle eyes seeking mine, I would do the same, and more.

*   *   *   *

Mr. Rennishawe was a man of his word. When he struck it was hard, and soon, and in a way that would hurt. At noon the next day a letter was delivered into my Father's hands. It told him that as his infirmities were now such as to make him unfit for employment, he was required to quit the cottage that day week on pain of imprisonment.

There is no entry in my diary for the days that followed. I was too heartsick for such things. What cut me most was that they had not reproached me. Father's face had told all he felt when he read that letter; but to me he only said, 'Angus, man, pride will be your downfa'.' And Mother, from whom I had taken the home she had come to as a bride, and where her children had been born, only turned away and went quickly into the kitchen, a great clattering of pots drowning the sound of her weeping.

When Father read the Scriptures aloud that night, as he always did, he chose the Hundred and Twenty First Psalm.

'I will lift up mine eyes unto the hills, from whence cometh my help; My help cometh even from the Lord, who hath made Heaven and earth. He will not suffer thy foot to be moved; and he that keepeth thee will not sleep.'

But the Lord, as Mother reminded us sharply when her first tears were dry, helps those who help themselves. Before all things came the need to find a place to go in which Father could be nursed and I and Fiona find some work.

'Ailie!' she cried triumphantly. 'Ailie will let us

stay with her in Glasgow until we find a new hame.'
And a letter was dispatched to my Auntie that very
morning. But the thought was in all our minds: what
was I, the breadwinner, to do in Glasgow? How could
a countryman live there by the skills that were his?
And even if I were to work as a docker or a labourer,
how could I earn enough to keep my parents, unless
Fiona were to earn a handsome wage?

I put my head in my hands and groaned when I
thought of all these things, and of what I had done
to my ain folk.

Auntie Ailie answered by the next post. She would
be glad, she said, to put us up for a time, if we did
not mind sleeping a wee thought crowded, I with
Donald, who still lodged with her, Fiona with Auntie,
and Mother and Father in the one spare room. And
so we began the sad task of packing up what things
we could take with us: little enough.

'The table can go to Mistress McLeish,' said my
Mother, pretending she could bear to part with what
her own father had made for her as a marriage gift.
'I'd like to think o't in a place I kent.' Then her eyes
filled and she busied herself with the packing.

When I came home for my supper on the Tuesday
(my dismissal had been on the Friday before) her face
was almost as bright as it used to be. She ran out to
meet me, full of news.

'Here's an unco' thing, Angus! Come and sit doon
while I tell ye.'

That morning, she said, as she had been hanging
out washing, the Castle dog-cart had stopped by our
gate. One of the grooms was driving, and at first
Mother did not recognise the lady who sat beside him.
Then she saw that it was Mrs Rennishawe, for once
not muffled up in scarves, but wearing a summer
costume and a smart straw hat. Mother, in her apron
with her sleeves rolled up and her face flushed from
bending over the tub, hardly knew where to put herself

when the laird's lady descended from the dog-cart and approached the cottage. Mother bobbed a curtsey, which Mrs Rennishawe acknowledged graciously.

'Will ye no' come in, ma'am?' asked my Mother. The invitation was accepted, and I can guess from Mother's account that the conversation went something like this.

'Can I offer ye a cup, ma'am? The kettle's on the boil.'

'Thank you, no — I breakfasted late.' The lady's eyes took in the room, the boxes and baskets full of packed clothes and possessions, and (I suspect) my Mother's red eyes.

'I — I came to ask you a favour,' she said hesitantly (drawing a pattern on the floor with the neb of her parasol, said my Mother). 'I wonder if, when you go from here — you would be prepared to leave your daughter with me?'

My Mother said that she almost fell backwards into the washing-tub with astonishment. But she managed to lower herself into a chair instead, forgetting her apron and her sleeves in listening to Mrs Rennishawe's praise of Fiona, her willingness, her neat hands, her quickness of mind. 'She is fit for any society, and I would like to train her in my own ways. And I think, though possibly I should not say it' — she smiled faintly — 'there is an attachment between Miss Hudson and our young footman, Robert.'

It was the first Mother had heard of it. But she managed to calm her whirling thoughts and to assure Mrs Rennishawe that nothing would give her greater pleasure, not to mention the solving of one of the family's difficulties in the forthcoming removal. She shepherded Mrs Rennishawe round to the little kitchen garden where Father was sitting in the sun, a plaid over his knees; and the good news had to be told to him, and received gladly, before Mrs Rennishawe looked at the little enamel watch pinned to her blouse with a golden knot, and said that she must go. At the gate she paused, and looked at them, Mother said, like one of their own kind, no longer stiff and haughty.

'I wish you well,' she said, 'very well.' And she turned and hurried back to the dog-cart.

'I never kent before what a kindly, bonny lady she was,' said Mother. 'It's my guess her family are a sair cross for her to bear.'

Then, all glee again, she pointed out to us that one problem had been solved by a miracle. I had never been much of a Kirk attender, except by compulsion, but I put up a wee prayer of thanks that night before I slept.

Even now, with the evidence all around me, I can hardly believe that another miracle followed the first. Two days had passed, during which our spirits fell again. It was Thursday evening. I was scraping my boots outside, having walked through a boggy patch to fetch back a strayed hen-bird. Mother had called me in to supper, laid ready on the dear, condemned table. I could hear her tempting Father to eat, for he had little appetite.

'Just a bit of trout, Ian, fresh this morning. Tammas caught it himsel'. It'll do ye guid.'

I was listening for his reply and did not hear footsteps behind me, so that I started with surprise when an English voice said, 'Good evening.' The speaker was a stranger, a gentleman in clothes that had cost as much as a year or more of my wages. He was tall, and would have seemed taller but for a stoop of the shoulders, and about Father's age, with some grey in his hair and moustache. He smiled, and I suddenly recognised the face of the gentleman who had looked kindly at me as I had stormed out of Mr Rennishawe's library.

'We've met before, I think,' he said, 'though not formally introduced. Southwold.'

I stammered some sort of greeting to Mr Southwold.

'Your parents at home?' he asked. I nodded dumbly.

'May I come in?' Gracefully, without waiting for my reply, he drifted into the cottage, causing Mother and Father to pause in their meal with forks half-way to their mouths, like folk receiving an angelic visitation; which, as it turned out, they were. Father rose painfully to offer the visitor a chair. He accepted it and sat beaming amiably on us.

'Pray continue your meal,' he said. 'I must apologise for interrupting it. No, thank you, I'll not partake myself. I must keep my appetite for dinner.'

'You're verra welcome, sir,' said my Mother. 'No' juist a cup of tea?'

'Well, thank you, since you press me.' He sipped it courteously, with little pretence of drinking. 'May I introduce myself? Southwold. Lord Southwold,' he added, with a twinkle in my direction. 'I would not have called at such an inconvenient time had the matter not been urgent. Your son and I have met before, Mr Hudson, though briefly. I was present last Friday when he—ah—expressed himself somewhat freely to my host, Mr Rennishawe.' I felt myself blushing violently. 'Now it appeared to me that although his language was not, perhaps, altogether Parliamentary, there was a certain justification for it.'

'Aye, we're wi' you there, sir,' put in Father loyally.

'I am not myself a man for field sports,' went on Lord Southwold, crossing his legs comfortably. 'On the whole I prefer Scotland out of season, as at present, when one is not being perpetually deafened by guns going off in one's ear. One shoots, of course, 'but—' He waved away any pleasure there might be in shooting. 'However, I do know a good gun-dog when I see one, and I am particularly fond of dogs of all kinds. Too fond, my wife thinks. And while I appreciate that they must occasionally be destroyed, I have very strong objections to their being hanged. Or to anybody being hanged, if it comes to that. Has it

82

occurred to you, Mr Hudson, that only eight years ago the barbaric practice of hanging criminals publicly was discontinued? I said in the Lords at the time . . . but dear me, I'm digressing. What I came to say to you is that I feel that your son here is not only an excellent gamekeeper but a man of principle.'

I blushed even harder. I had never thought of myself as a man of principle, or even as a man. I felt older then and there; such is the value of praise.

'It happens,' went on His Lordship, 'that I am in need of a gamekeeper and ghillie on my estate in Perthshire. A cottage goes with the post—rather larger than this one, I seem to remember.' He gazed thoughtfully about our poor despoiled living-room. Then his gaze returned to me. 'Would you consider such an appointment, Mr Angus?'

Would I consider it! With joy and gratitude I accepted the wonderful offer then and there, and shook Lord Southwold's hand on it. So did my parents, until that good man's hand must have been sore. The rest of his visit is a misty blur in my memory, but I recall that arrangements were made for us and our belongings to travel to Lord Southwold's estate of Glenbryde, between the Braes o' Doune and Allan Water. I trust we thanked him adequately; I believe we did. We Scots are poor at uttering our feelings, but our hearts speak volumes through our eyes.

Lord Southwold bade us a cordial goodnight, and departed. I watched him as he went. He drew a book from his pocket and began to read as he walked, his head bent in a scholar's stoop. So ended happily my first encounter with Hugo Talbot-Carey, Earl of Southwold, whom I was to serve proudly in the years to come.

CHAPTER EIGHT

10 July, 1876

'Surely the lot is fallen to us in pleasant places.'
The text comes into my mind often these days.

We have been a month at Glenbryde. It is much
smaller than Invermore, being maintained more for
the benefit of His Lordship's friends than himself, I
am told. This Perthshire country is most beautiful,
filled with great mountains famous in story and forests
where the red deer roam. Here King James wandered
in the guise of a lowly knight to see how his people
lived, and Roderick Dhu led Clan Alpine into battle
to the sound of the war-pipes. The folk here speak
with the same soft Highland voice as Grandmother,
and in the wild regions they talk as freely of fairies
and goblins as Lowlanders do of mutton and coals.
To hear them, you would think it was hardly safe to
walk alone for fear of meeting the evil Kelpie, the
river-horse who comes from the depths of the loch
to steal maidens and children, or the Noontide Hag,
the Glaslich, a terrible female spectre who haunts
Knoidart. Then there is the Ban-Shie, who screams all
night before the death of a chieftain, and the ghostly
horses of the McLeans. I am glad not to be of a
superstitious turn of mind.

But in Glenbryde House it is mostly English voices
I hear. At first I found them hard to follow, for they
speak so quickly and some in a strange and ugly
accent which I am told is London Cockney. His Lordship is away now, taking part in a debate in the
House of Lords. They say he is a great politician, and
might one day be Prime Minister, but his heart is in
his English home and in his books. Father and he

have long talks about literary matters, and I can see that it takes Father's mind off his pain.

Lady Southwold is a braw woman with a fine shape and a head of hair on her like polished chestnut-wood, but her tongue is sharp and her eyes keen as a sparrowhawk's. There is a daughter, Lady Marjorie, and a son, Viscount Ashby, at Eton College. I almost dread their coming to Glenbryde, when I remember the Rennishawes.

Our own cottage is—

There my diary broke at some interruption. But I do not need any reminder of that wee house, so much pleasanter than the old one. Our parlour looked away to the east on one side and to the west on the other, so that its windows caught the rising and setting sun. There was a better bedroom for my parents, and for me a spacious loft with a view of mountain, burn and forest that the Queen herself might envy.

In some strange way, although we were farther away from the towns than we had been at Invermore, we seemed to be nearer to Glasgow and even to England. When Lord Southwold came North he would stroll over after dinner to have a crack with Father, and perhaps a dram and a smoke, and tell us what was going on at the seat of government. So we heard at first hand that Her Majesty had become Empress of India through the power of her wily minister, Benjamin Disraeli, Lord Beaconsfield, leader of His Lordship's party, and how she had put aside her widow's blacks and sat at table glistering with Eastern gems. We learned of the terrible war between Russia and Turkey, and the outbreak of the second Afghan war. Lord Southwold told us how his old leader had travelled to Germany and engineered the signing of the Congress of Berlin, which was to keep Europe from war for many years to come; and how, when he returned with the triumphant slogan "Peace with Honour!' had been cheered by the crowds outside his house in Downing Street, a bent figure with hair and beard dyed jetty black.

'We're all growing old,' said the Earl with a sigh to my Father. 'I'm not so young as I used to be, I can tell you. I shall keep a footing at Westminster while Dizzy lasts, and then—ah, sweet retirement!'

'That would be a great waste of Your Lordship's powers,' my Father told him. 'It's such as you we need to keep Britain steady, with changes all around us, and no' for the better.'

His Lordship laughed. 'My dear Hudson, you mustn't be retrograde. Many of the new things are going to make us more comfortable than we've ever been—and keep us amused. You must hear this marvellous whatsitsname, phonograph. American fellow called Edison patented it this year. Deuced clumsy thing, but they'll improve that. Why don't you come up and hear it tomorrow night? I don't think we're expecting other company.'

Father's face was wistful, for he dearly loved a jaunt; but he could scarcely walk ten paces now on his crippled legs. Lord Southwold read his thoughts. 'I'll send the gig for you about eight,' he said casually.

And promptly at eight the trim wee carriage was at our door, with Sidgwick the coachman ready to hoist Father up beside him. Away they went, the few hundred yards up to the House, Mother and I on foot behind.

I had been inbye several times before, with messages to the Family, but never a real guest, invited to sit down and be entertained. I felt my best breeches were not good enough for my leather-cushioned chair, and from the expression on her face I guessed Her Ladyship agreed with me. I had learned at Invermore that the English nobility in general do not hob-nob with ordinary folk, but expect bobs and curtseys and other servilities from us. We Scots are too proud for that, I am happy to say. Though I felt like a bullock in a bower, as Mother would say, I met the Countess's eye straight and unflinching, not as a social equal but as a fellow-human. After a while she permitted herself a smile, and from that evening she never again gave me orders in the sharp voice she used to other tenants.

We sat in the Library, which His Lordship told us was his favourite room. The walls were lined with books, hundreds of them by my count; but not, he said, anything like the number he had at Southwold in England. I knew him by now well enough to be aware that he would, given the choice, rather have been reading in his favourite armchair than amusing us, and yet was made happy by our happiness. He was a great statesman and a great gentleman; and, forbye, he still is.

I cannot attempt to describe the instrument His Lordship proudly wound up before our fascinated eyes. We must have looked like three bunnies under the spell of a weasel, when sounds began to come from the object that were without doubt human: a man was speaking faintly against crackling noises something like bursts of gunfire. The voice came and went in eerie waves, producing an effect which would not, I felt, have disgraced the Noontide Hag and the Ban-Shie.

'It fair makes my bluid run cold,' said Mother with a shudder. Father's bemused face was suddenly illuminated, and he began to recite in time with the ghostly voice.

'. . . this blessed plot, this earth, this realm,
            this England,
This nurse, this teeming womb of royal kings
Feared by their breed, and famous by their
            birth . . .'

He broke off to explain triumphantly:

87

'King Richard the Second! By William Shakespeare. Act Two!'

'Oh, is *that* what it is?' said Her Ladyship in languid tones. But I noticed a certain respect dawn in her eye for my Father's scholarship.

When the man ceased a woman's voice began to sing in a high screech which was not at all agreeable, but wonderful to hear for all that.

'Nation shall speak peace unto nation,' quoted Father.

His Lordship nodded. 'We live in wondrous times.' Then, to the Countess, 'My dear, do you think a little refreshment—?' She turned a small gold handle by the side of the marble fireplace. In less than a minute the door opened, and a manservant appeared.

'You rang, Your Ladyship?' he asked in very English accents.

'Tea, Widgery.'

'Perhaps something a little stronger for you, Hudson?' suggested His Lordship. Father indicated that if it were no trouble he would partake of something stronger with pleasure. 'The Courvoisier '68, Widgery,' Lord Southwold told the butler. Widgery reappeared with a silver tray, bearing elegant tea-cups and saucers and also a decanter of what Father told me later was a brandy so fine that to drink it seemed a kind of desecration.

I did not take kindly to Mr Widgery at first sight, and my further acquaintance with him did nothing to cause me to change my mind. It is hard for a Southron like him to deceive those who have spent their lives in the free air under open skies, and I saw that for all his servile manner before his employers, he would be a very different man in the servants' hall. He had the eye of a tyrant and the lips of a lecher: I have seen a bust of the Emperor Nero with just such a mouth on him.

But beside my dislike of the man grew a respect

for his office. He seemed to be Lord Southwold's deputy, head of the household as His Lordship was head of the Family and the Castle. At Invermore I had taken little notice of the butler; now, in this smaller establishment, he appeared to me a figure of great power and responsibility. I felt that Lord Southwold deserved a better man than Widgery to serve him. I even dared to dream that I might serve him myself in just that capacity, rather than as a mere keeper on his estate.

I saw little of Mr Widgery. He had no love for the outdoor life, and little for living things. I knew that he feared horses, and once I caught him kicking a dog that had jumped up at him. On another occasion I went to the dairy for our milk, to interrupt a scene of struggle between him and the dairymaid Katrine, a lass of no more than fourteen. When I appeared at the door Mr Widgery released her, very red in the face, and stalked out past me. He never forgave me for that incident.

Time passed. I see its milestone as I turn over the pages of my diaries.

8 December, 1879

Today I rode into Doune to fetch the doctor to Father, who is in great pain. He has not closed his eyes these three nights past, nor Mother either. The doctor said there was nothing to be done for him but keep him warm and give him laudanum to help him sleep. The house is warm, Lady Southwold having a great dislike of chills and damp for herself and her tenants, but nothing seems to warm Father's bones.

The snow has come early. Jamie the shepherd and I and others have brought the sheep down into the meadow beyond the Family's garden, and enclosed it with double fencing. Foxes are coming down from the hills to steal the kitchen stuff, and the deer from Findhu Glen have grown tame enough to touch. It is said that the Family will not be coming to Glenbryde for Christmas and Hogmanay. Mr Widgery and most of the staff have gone to Southwold, the rest to find winter work in the towns. I think it will be but a sad Hogmanay.

22 December

Fiona has come from Invermore as cantie as a lamb in Spring, bonnier than ever. Young Robert Wilson's ring is on her finger, and they are to marry in three months. Though he is but a footman now, she says he has great ambitions to get into the hotel trade and work his way up to manager.

Between the leaves of my diary is a printed card edged with black. My heart sinks at the sight of it; for before Fiona had married her beau, Father was dead.

He had been well during the day, full of pleasure to see the green grass coming out from the snow covering of that long harsh winter. He had sat propped up on his parlour couch, reading with pleasure from the books Lord Southwold had left him: that day I think it was Boswell's *Journal of a Tour to the Hebrides with Doctor Johnson*. When it was time for bed he said to Mother, who sat in her rocking-chair with her eyes closed:

'Gang awa' upstairs, Margaret. I'm fine and drowsy, I'll need nothing the nicht.'

She was hard to persuade, but at last she agreed to leave the little wall-bed, where she usually slept, for the comfortable bedroom. We said goodnight to him together. I turned at the door for a last look at him in the firelight, smiling and raising one crippled hand in a salute.

When we came down next morning he still smiled, but in the sleep of death, all the lines of pain smoothed from his face, the Hebridean Journal open on the floor as though it had slipped from his hand as he dozed off.

I cannot think he hastened his end with the sleeping-draught, though it lay within his reach. The doctor inclined to think that the moment had come for his heart to stop; a merciful end to suffering. He was only forty-eight years old.

We missed him sorely. From that day Mother seemed smaller and slower, and I knew that I carried a man's burdens on my shoulders.

More milestones are reached, and passed, The home-coming of Lady Marjorie, a beautiful girl just turned twenty, with her Mother's bonnie hair but a soft hazel eye, and as kind a heart as her Daddy's. Her brother, Hugo, Lord Ashby, was a tall handsome lad, as pleasant-spoken as herself. There was nothing in them to remind me of the Rennishawes, I gave thanks. I liked them fine, the two young folk, and Glenbryde was a happier place for their coming.

9 July, 1880

Donald has left Glasgow University with flying colours. He is a Bachelor of Science, my wee brother, and is to go abroad immediately with an engineering firm with a contract to build a dam in Egypt. He came to see us yesterday, a well-grown young man, no longer, as Mother said, as roond as a haggis, and so like me in feature and colouring that she continually looked from one to the other of us with hands upraised in wonder. As he left us he wrung my hand until I winced for the pain of it.

'I'll never forget what you did for me, Angus,' he said. 'Not if I live to be as old as Methuselah.'

'Why, what did I do so remarkable?' I asked him, and indeed I had no idea.

'You stood aside for me,' he said. 'Two roads lay before us, and you took the narrow one and left me the braid highway. Maybe you canna see it now, but you will. I wish you—' and there his voice broke and he turned and almost ran down the path to our gate.

I went about my work as usual, whistling to keep up my spirits, until I realised what the tune was, and Rabbie's sad words came into my mind.

> 'This night is my departing night,
>   For here nae langer must I stay;
> There's neither friend nor foe of mine
>   But wishes, wishes me away.
> What I hae done through lack of wit
>   I never, never can recall;
> I hope ye're a' my friends as yet:
>   Goodnight, and joy be wi' ye a'.'

I knew that it was daft to be sad, that my brother was starting on a grand career. Yet one by one my folk were leaving me, and I knew in my heart that it would be many years before I met Donald again.

That same month marks another milestone. In April Lord Beaconsfield's government had fallen. He had been staying in Hatfield at the time of the election, and when he heard that his Tory-Democrat party was defeated he said to his host's eldest son: 'This is the beginning of your political life, but it is the end of mine.'

It was also the end of Lord Southwold's. True to his words, he retired from politics rather than serve under the Liberals and Mr Gladstone. 'My family,' he said to me when I called to welcome him home, 'my family, Hudson, have given five Prime Ministers to the nation. Now I think that's quite enough, don't you?' and added in French something which I asked him to render into English for me (being always anxious to increase my knowledge.)

'It means,' he said, 'that sometimes it is necessary to cultivate one's garden. That is exactly what I pro-

pose to do. I shall remain here until the end of the
season to give my friends a little pleasure and prove
to myself that I can still shoot straight, and then—
who knows? Next Spring we may all find ourselves
in different circumstances, eh, what?'

Next Spring, the twenty-fifth of my young life,
would bring me—oh, Lindsay, Lindsay!

CHAPTER NINE

There is something folded in paper between the pages, as I turn them. I know what I shall see when I unwrap it, and hesitate whether or not to leave it hidden. Almost without my direction my fingers lay open the flimsy wrappings, and I see with a pain as sweet and sharp as ever it was what is within.

It is a locket-case, a small oval of leather rubbed rough by contact with my pocket, for I used to carry it with me everywhere. The photograph inside has been coloured by the hand of a photographer in unnatural tints: the hair is chocolate-brown, the lips and cheeks the colour of ripe strawberries. Yet in it I see the living image of my long-dead love: a rosy face, eyes dark as a hill-tarn, hair of shining black, ready to fall in a tangle of curls but severely confined in a knot at the nape of her white neck. There is a look on her of somebody else; my Grandmother Morag, whose great-niece she was. Lindsay MacLeod of Skye.

She came to Glenbryde in August, 1880, when the shooting season was in full spate and I was out every day, acting as loader to Lord Southwold (Mr Widgery, whose duty it was, had been struck down by an attack of gout, the result, I erroneously suspected, of furtive indulgence in his employer's port.) Mother felt her lonely situation very much, Father dead, Donald overseas, and Fiona away to England with her bridegroom to work in a London hotel. She tried not to pain me with her sadness, saying 'I'm no' dreich, Angus, it's auld age loupin' on apace.'

'That for a tale,' I returned. 'Man wasna made to

bide alone, nor was woman. I'll just sit down and write to Auntie Ailie.'

'No, dinna do that. Ailie's no' young hersel' and this place would never suit her after Glesca'. It would be cruel to bring her. Yet I'd like fine some company . . .' She pondered. 'There's your Father's cousin Lachlan—son to your Nannie's Brother Donuil. No, his bairns were baith laddies.' Her eye brightened. But there's Lachlan's sister Flora, wha married a MacLeod of Skye. She had lasses, I mind. Maybe one of them would be glad to lend a hand at Glenbryde and bide here.'

I lost no time in writing to Auntie Flora, whom I had never seen. With Highland courtesy she replied at once, saying that her elder daughter Marie was to be wed in the Autumn but that the younger one, Lindsay, was free and would enjoy travel and change. She was, Auntie added, only seventeen but capable of any work from fine needlework to milking a cow. The only difficulty was religion: as a Roman Catholic she would have to ask us to undertake that Lindsay would be conveyed to a Catholic church every Sunday. If that were guaranteed she would be ready to come to us at once.

I assured Auntie that I myself would see that she was taken in the trap to the nearest church of her Faith, at Doune, a few miles away. Several folk round Glenbryde were of the old religion, so that she would find plenty of company.

I met her at Callander a week later. She had travelled that long journey partly by road and partly by the new railway that was bringing the great world to the Highlands. It was a journey which might have tired out the strongest man, but there was no trace of fatigue upon her when she stepped from the little train at Callander station. Her little hat was askew and her hair tumbling down; there were smuts on her wild-rose face and her cotton gloves were black from the dirt of the train, but to me she was a vision of such beauty as I had never seen. The sun had set behind great Ben Ledi, away in the west. I remember that in my daze at the first sight of her I drew out my watch and consulted it, at which she laughed, saying 'I am not late, am I? The train came at a fair gallop.' My confusion was doubled, for her Highland speech was strange and at first incomprehensible to me, being so much more foreign than the accent of Perthshire. I must have looked a gaby, staring at her with my watch in my hand. It was not until she asked me to help her with her baggage that I came to myself.

As we drove to Glenbryde, jogging behind the stout little mare, Maggie, Lindsay rattled on about the excitements of her journey, the beautiful scenery, the interesting passengers, the delight and wonder of it all. I thought of a picture I had seen in some book, of blessed souls arriving in Paradise with outstretched arms and joyful faces. My Cousin might well have been one of them.

I was angry with myself because I could think of nothing to say. She would think me a stupid great gowk, I told myself furiously, and strove to put in intelligent remarks suitable to the kind of worldly-wise person I had earlier felt myself to be. It was a relief when she fell silent, looking round her at the beautiful Braes o' Doune. I told her their name, at which she sang softly:

'Ye banks and braes o' bonnie Doon,
    How can ye bloom sae fresh and fair?'

Then she asked me were these the same braes, and I was ashamed of myself because I could not tell her. Maybe they were and then again maybe they were not, I murmured. She hummed the tune, and I managed to keep one eye on Maggie, who was inclined to pause and crop wayside grass, and the other on Lindsay. I cannot tell now what she wore, except that it was a neat-fitting costume of tweed, and that the colour of it seemed sometimes purple and sometimes green in the changing light. I felt the evening peace calming me, so that I could speak to her without my voice sounding strange in my ears.

'Yon's an unco' name—Lindsay. I never heard of a lassie called that before.'

'It's a woman's name as much as a man's. Do you not like it?'

'I like it fine. Lindsay MacLeod . . .'

She looked up at me, smiling. 'I like yours—but for the Hudson. If you were not my cousin I should have to call you Mr Hudson.' She made a face. 'That's a real Sassenach name. Have you the Gaelic, Aengus?' (that was how my name sounded on her lips.)

I had to confess that I had not one word of it, on which she rattled off a string of words quite incomprehensible to me, though I seemed to hear among them some I had heard from my Grandmother. I asked her what she had said, to which she replied straight-faced:

'A thousand blessings on your house; may your cows give as much milk in a year as Loch Scavaig holds of water, and your sheep be as many as white clouds over the Cuillins.'

Then, seeing my face fall because I thought her mocking me for my ignorance, she said sweetly:

'It is a blessing to be spoken when coming for the first time to the house of a friend.'

A blessing she proved to be in herself, for Mother's days were lightened by her presence. A cheerful face and a silver laugh, a ready hand to any task had Lindsay. She seemed to have no regret for her island home, though she wrote often to her Mother and told us many tales of the Isles: of the fairy flag of the

MacLeods, of a man of Skye more than a hundred years old who recalled his Father wearing a crape armband in mourning for the death of Prince Charlie in 1788, and had talked with men who had been out in the '45.

Sometimes in the evenings she would bring out the *clarsach*, the little Gaelic harp, and sing to us such songs as we had never heard since the death of Grandmother: songs of stolen children and fairy changelings, of warring chiefs and exiled men, of the boats, the fishing, weaving and herding that were the Hebridean trades.

It was not long before Mother declared that her spirits were now so improved that she could no longer keep Lindsay at home all day. At Glenbryde House they were short of a dairymaid, for Katrine had left after the day when I had surprised Mr Widgery trying to assault her. I was not too happy about Lindsay running the risk of a similar attack, and I told her plainly what I had seen, but she laughed.

'A pity it would be if I could not hold off an old fat man the like of him!' and she braced her sturdy young arms to show how strong they were. I was doubtful, but as it turned out Mr Widgery left her alone, I suspect because he enjoyed terrorising young women, and knew that she was one who would not be bullied. She had been used to dairy work at home, milking her Mother's cows and making butter and cheese, so it was only sensible that she should do so at Glenbryde and earn herself money besides. She seemed to have a magic hand with cows, quieting the most nervous of them by her touch and her voice, singing softly to them the milking song of the Isles, *Colin's Cattle*, to make them give good milk in plenty.

It was on a winter's night, as we walked together back from the dairy to our cottage, that I asked her to marry me. My heart was beating so fast that I thought she would hear it, for fear she should not accept me. But she raised her eyes to mine, saying, 'Yes, Angus,' as though there was no other answer she could have given.

Mother knew at once, when we came in, what had happened. As I have said, we were not a demonstrative family, but she put her arms first round me and then round Lindsay, calling her daughter.

I had never been as happy as I was that winter. I did not know such happiness was possible. It was a mild season, the leaves staying on the trees until late November, the heather as richly purple on the mountains as when it first bloomed. We walked together along the burnside every day when we were free of work, talking of the life we would have, even of our children that would be. I learnt a few words of love from her, *mo chridhe,* my dear, *m'eudail,* my darling, and she some Lowland words from me, which sounded so strange in her lilting voice that she said them over and over to make me laugh, for she said I was too serious for my age.

It was arranged that she should travel home for Christmas and Hogmanay, and return in time to prepare for our wedding in March. Mother was happy that we should share the cottage. 'I thocht ye were no' the marrying kind, Angus,' she said. 'It was never in my mind that I should nurse bairns of yours.' And indeed I had never thought of myself as the marrying kind. I could scarcely believe my fortune in gaining a wife; and such a wife as Lindsay.

When she had gone the time seemed endless to me, though it passed pleasantly enough, without snow or ice. There was gloomy talk that a green Yule made a fat kirkyard, but to my thinking that was daft. Our farm beasts were spared starvation and death from cold, our game-birds were not the prey of hungry foxes, and Lady Southwold's temper was the sweeter for the warmth that made Glenbryde possible to live in (though she spent as much time as possible in London).

In February my darling came back. She and Mother fell into a spate of work, sewing curtains and coverlets for the part of the cottage which was to be ours, making dresses and other things I was not allowed to see for Lindsay's bridal, and shopping in Doune for furnishings which would make our rooms fresh and cheerful. We were to be married at the Catholic church of Doune, because Lindsay could not by the articles of her faith wed anywhere else. Mother was not pleased about this, nor was I free of some kind of guilt at abandoning the Kirk I had attended all my life (though, as I have said, I was not very religious). Father Aloysius rode up from Doune, and proved to be so congenial that Mother's disapproval faded somewhat, only to return when she learnt that any children we might have would be brought up Catholics.

Father Aloysius had a sharp eye. Patting Mother's shoulder, he said, 'It goes against the grain, Mistress Hudson. But do you not think a daughter-in-law the like of Miss MacLeod is worth a few scruples?'

He said it so comically that despite her feelings Mother had to laugh, after which we all, even Lindsay whose favourite drink was buttermilk, took a dram for goodwill's sake, and the Father and I took a second, which moved me to sing *Auld Lang Syne* so feelingly that Lindsay collapsed in laughter and had to go into the kitchen to recover herself.

I see a fateful entry in my diary for 1881.

26 February

Lindsay is not well. This morning she complained of a sore throat and an uneasy feeling in her bones. I took word to the dairy that she would not be at work today; Mhairi and Hamish will do her tasks. I think she has maybe a cold coming on, not the

100

influenza, I hope. They have had it in England, but so far it has not troubled us up here.

This evening I took her a celandine flower I had picked, the first of the Spring. Her face was much flushed, and she seemed at first not to know me, which made me sad, but I knew it was her state. She has hot bricks wrapped in flannel to her feet and Mother's herb brew to drink as hot as she can bear it.

27 February

Lindsay was a little better this morning. Later she seemed improved in herself, but Mother has found red blotches on her chest and neck, and her brow is very hot.

At four o'clock I went for Doctor McAlister. He said little but that we should keep her in bed. She asked what day was it, and wept when I told her. 'Shall I not be well for our wedding?' she asked me, holding tight to my hands.

28 February

Doctor McAlister came again. Three of Keeper Macintyre's bairns are ill with the same fever Lindsay has. They are out in spots, which have now appeared on her.

Doctor McAlister says it is the measles, a childish complaint very rife when the winter has been mild. Frost and snow kill the infection, which thrives on warmth. It is not serious, he says, especially at Lindsay's age.

I cannot read the next entry. I remember every letter of it, and every pang I felt.

That night she did not know either Mother or me, and talked ramblingly of her childhood and the cattle. Her brow was burning hot. We put cold compresses to it but the feverish heat did not abate. She cried out that the light hurt her eyes, and we drew the blind and hung a dark cloth round the lamp. Her voice was a hoarse croak; a tearing cough racked her. She managed to say that she could hardly breathe, even when Mother propped her up on three pillows.

When the rash became a darkish purple, covering her face and body, I rode again for the doctor. This time he exclaimed with horror when he saw her. She had the disease in its most malignant form, he said, one that occurs frequently in a healthy person who had lived in a community free from infections, as Lindsay had done. He told Mother to pile blankets on her to help her sweat out the fever and to boil water so that she could inhale the steam. But she tossed and turned so much that we could not hold the basin steady.

After an hour he asked me to stable his horse for the night, and when I came back ordered me to bed, as Mother had told him I had not slept for three nights. I protested, but he said, 'You'll do her no good by wearying yourself. Get along, now.'

As I went out of the room I heard Mother say to him, 'Her brow is cooler', and my mind eased a little. Crazed as I was for sleep I fell upon my bed and knew nothing more, until I awoke shivering with cold, and saw that it was growing light. I dragged my stiff limbs downstairs, thinking to make a pot of tea to warm myself up. The whole house was quiet. When I entered the kitchen I was amazed to find Mother there, sitting at the table with her head on her arms. She looked up, and I saw in her face what had happened.

I made to go back upstairs, but she rose and held me back. I found that I could not speak, merely shake my head from side to side. Then I managed to say 'But the fever was less . . .'

'That was the onset of the crisis,' said Mother. 'She didna come through it.'

And so we buried my Lindsay a week before she should have married me, in the graveyard of the little Catholic church, and Father Aloysius celebrated the

Mass for the Dead. It troubled him that he had not reached Lindsay in time to administer the Last Rites and hear her confession. I almost laughed in his face in my bitterness. What had she to confess, poor innocent? Mother laid her own wedding-veil over Lindsay's face as she lay in her coffin; and before it was closed I put her little harp in beside her, knowing that I could never bear to look on it or hear it again.

*　*　*　*

For some six weeks I went about my work like a man in a bad dream. I believe folk showed great kindness to me and Mother, but I must have seemed sullen and ungrateful, for I had nothing to say to them in return. His Lordship came to see us on the day after the funeral, and I seem to remember that he stammered slightly as he spoke words of sympathy, and that Mother apologised for the smell of the disinfectant fluid from the sheets hung over the doors to keep the infection from spreading.

What did I think of during that black time? I longed to get away from Glenbryde, where everything reminded me of Lindsay and the happiness that should have been mine. The paths where we walked, the views which had charmed her, were all painful to me. I could not enter our cottage without my eyes going to the inglenook, where she had sat sewing or reading; at every homecoming it seemed to me that if I opened the door quickly enough I would surprise her gentle ghost before it had time to fade, and she would come running to embrace me as she always did. I no longer went to the dairy for our butter and milk, but sent one of the ghillies instead. I was foolishly angry with poor Mother because she put on a good face and chattered about little matters to cheer me. With shame I heard my surly answers and saw her face fall. Then I would go up to Lindsay's empty room and sit there, hoping in my sinfulness that I might catch the same fever and follow her.

I had thoughts of taking the Queen's shilling and going overseas to toss away my life in battle. But there was peace now in Afghanistan and General Roberts had come home. There was another reason for my restiveness. During that mild, damp winter I had begun to feel the same ache and stiffness in my bones that Father had complained of when his illness began. If I continued in my present way of life I would be a cripple in ten years.

But 'there's a Providence that shapes our ends, Rough-hew them as we will.' Little though I deserved it, that Providence was watching over me.

When Lord Southwold sent for me after a month's absence in London I neither guessed nor cared the purpose of his summons. But I was surprised to see Her Ladyship with him. Both gave me a friendly greeting, and no mention was made of my loss, only talk of the late Spring and of the fishing for which Lord Southwold had come to Scotland. Then he reached the point of his summons.

'Hudson,' he said, 'you may or may not know that I am giving up Glenbryde.' I had not heard; even in my crazy state, I should have remembered the fact.

'Now that I have retired from politics,' he went on, 'I feel it is quite unnecessary to keep on three establishments—our London house, Southwold and Glenbryde.'

'Ridiculous, in fact,' put in Her Ladyship, who had never troubled to conceal her dislike for the Scottish climate.

'I do not propose to sell Glenbryde at once, but to lease it for a year or so. Now, Hudson, we come to the point: Lord Strathallan, who will be taking it over in August, is prepared to keep on any of the local staff who may wish to stay with him, which I imagine will be the majority. But—' breaking off, he looked at his wife appealingly. 'I really think you had better

104

continue, my dear.' He rose and strolled to the window, from which he appeared to contemplate the prospect. Lady Southwold leant towards me and spoke and looked more kindly than I had ever seen her.

'Hudson,' she said, 'you must know how deeply Lord Southwold and I have felt for you in your trouble. We have talked over the situation, in the light of the change to come, and we wonder if you would like to accompany us?'

I must have looked as dumbfounded as the Laird o' Cockpen, and even more so when she continued.

'We've no need of gamekeepers at Southwold (which is to be our principal home, by the way) but the present domestic staff are rather inadequate for such a big place. Do you feel you could take to the life of a footman, Hudson? It will be very unlike your present state, but we have both thought for some time that you had the appearance and the intelligence for a more social occupation than that of a gamekeeper.'

By this time I was blushing to such an extent that it would not have surprised me to see flames rising from my collar. I stuttered some sort of thanks.

'We shall be entertaining a great deal next season, not only our own friends but those of our son and daughter, so you would have more than enough employment.' I knew that Lady Southwold was tactfully implying that I would have little time for grieving. 'Widgery,' she went on, 'would train you thoroughly in your duties, of course. Oh, and if your mother wished to go with you I'm sure we could find something for her to do.'

His Lordship turned away from the window. 'Well, Hudson? what's the answer, eh?'

I could only say 'Thank you, my Lord. Thank you, my Lady. I'd like it fine.'

When I told Mother the news, wondering how she would take it, she relieved my mind by expressing joy at the prospect. 'I couldna stay here ma lane, and they'll be wanting the cottage for a new keeper. I've aye wanted to see new places, and there's nothing for either of us here, Angus.' Her face was excited and happy again. She laughed when I told her the end of the interview. As I was leaving, Lady Southwold called me back.

'One thing, Hudson—have you any other Christian name?'

'Roderick, my Lady,' I said. She frowned.

'Oh, dear. What a nuisance. Footmen in England must have easy English names. Names that won't confuse our foreign guests. John; have we got a John, Hugo?'

'Two, I believe, my dear.'

'Robert, then. No, that won't do. I can't bear the name for some reason. I have it—Charles! How would you fancy Charles, Hudson?'

'Very well, my Lady,' I replied in a voice that was already to my own ears beginning to sound like a footman's.

'Then that's splendid, Charles,' she said with satisfaction.

As I look on the last page in this old exercise book I see myself sitting, late on a summer night, in my room at Glenbryde. I see my clothes and effects packed in boxes, ready to be taken to the station. I see the black crape band on my arm as it rests on the table.

10 July, 1881

In a few hours I shall take my first steps into a different world. I see now that my path has led this way for many years. I never thought to become a liveried servant; yet there is a dignity in service which I shall always strive to maintain. May the Lord guide me in all my ways.

The old song runs in my head tonight that Lindsay

sang as I first drove her home to Glenbryde. *Ye banks and braes o' bonnie Doon, How can ye bloom sae fair? How can ye chant, ye little birds, And I sae fu' o' care?*

My chief of cares is going so far from Lindsay's grave. Yet go I must, at dawn tomorrow, to England.

CHAPTER TEN

15 July, 1882

This is a world of surprises. From the morn I left Glenbryde I have undergone one new experience after another, like a man entering a room to find a door leading into another room, from which leads yet a third door, and so on ad infinitum. I would not have dreamed that at my age—full twenty-six—I would be capable of such discovery and wonder. I shall never cease to bless Lord Southwold for taking me out of the Valley of the Shadow into new and pleasant lands.

Until five days ago I had never travelled by the railway further than Glasgow, and that seldom. I must admit that as our train passed through precipitous country I had uneasy recollections of the terrible Tay Bridge disaster only three years ago, when a North British Railway train was blown off the bridge by a high wind, and 73 persons drowned. What is a train, after all, but a frail thing of metal, man-constructed, in comparison with the mighty forces of Nature? But, happily, the train which conveyed our party met with no accidents.

I had no notion that special compartments for sleeping existed in railway trains, or that refreshment was served in transit. I sat with my eyes fixed on the changing landscapes that flitted past the window, the softness of the Lowland pastures and hills after our wild Highland mountains, the rugged Border country, and places which had so far been only names in a geography-book to me: Carlisle, where Prince Charlie's soldiers forded the Esk with a hundred pipers blowing them on, a glimpse of Hadrian's Wall, Shap Fell, Kendal and the mountains of the Lake District, so curiously unlike those of 'Scotland of the mist and storm'. We had passed through Kendal and were slowing up under the walls of Lancaster Castle and its neighbouring church, whose graveyard runs almost to the edge of the railway-line, before I fully realised that at last I was seeing England. The thought was as strange to me as if I had found myself in Australia or Fiji.

'It's as guid as a treat to watch your face, Angus,' said Mother, smiling. 'It minds me of when you were a wee laddie gawping at the cake-shop window. I could never get you past it withoot a battle.'

Town after town slipped by, each more industrial than the last, tall chimneys sending up smoke into the sky, which seemed to me greyer than any sky I had ever seen, just as the towns were uglier, little black houses built all to a pattern, mean streets and cinder wastelands. I thought maybe I was not going to take to England, all the more so when we came to the hideous kilns and slag-heaps which I was told were the main feature of the Potteries, the district in which porcelain and china of all sorts is made. It was somewhere about this point that my eyes closed in spite of myself, and I slept.

It was at Swindon that I awoke with a jolt, my neck exceedingly stiff and a taste in my mouth as if I had been chewing iron filings. Mr Widgery informed us that we were to alight at the station and would be taken to Southwold by road. He managed to convey with this information his utter disapproval of our presence in His Lordship's party, of my appointment as footman, and of my appearance and manners, while to Mother he hardly accorded the courtesy of a word; she would have been obliged to carry her own baggage had I not taken it from her. I sensed that whatever I might feel about England, I was not going to take to Mr Widgery. Nor, indeed, did I.

And so on a warm evening, covered with grit from

109

the journey (ah, Lindsay's small cotton gloves, train-soiled at Callender!), I set foot on English ground for the first time, and looked round the great bustling station.

'It's awfu' big,' said Mother. I had been about to make the same remark.

We were shepherded by Mr Widgery towards the station exit, where, in the forecourt, waited a handsome carriage with a coachman in smart livery. In this were accommodated Lord and Lady Southwold, Miss Dawson, Her Ladyship's maid, and Mr. Widgery. Mother and I and two young females who had been helping with the removal operations at Glenbryde occupied a smaller vehicle. They seemed as shy of us as we of them, so little conversation took place on the journey.

By this time we were very weary, both from the excitement of our new experiences and the extreme length of the journey. My head dropped sideways against the corner of the coach, and the beat of the horse's hooves lulled me into uneasy slumber. I did not know that we were travelling south-west through rural Wiltshire, away from the smoke and stench of Swindon though when I opened my leaden eyes now and then I was aware of open country and small neat villages, the windows glowing with lamplight as night fell. I had no notion how long the journey took. The two maids were also slumbering, one with her mouth unbecomingly open, and Mother's head rested on my shoulder. I was in the middle of a very unpleasant dream in which I was endeavouring to separate a ferocious wild cat from the old dog Luath, and getting painfully flung about as I wrestled with the two enraged animals, when Mr Widgery's voice once more roused me.

'Come on, can't you!' he barked. 'Or are you intending to stay there all night?'

'Where are we?' I asked dazedly, the visionary

110

combat receding and my injuries proving to be only the aches and stiffness from my cramped position in the coach.

'"Where are we?"'! he repeated in what was, I hope, a travesty of my Scots accent. 'We're at Southwold, that's where we are, and if you don't go about your business a bit smarter I shall have something to say to His Lordship.'

I preserved a dignified silence, helped out the three ladies, and followed Mr Widgery as he led the way to what was to be our home.

18 July

It seems strange to me after a lifetime of being housed in a gamekeeper's cottage to find myself in the great house itself. Until I came here I had never entered servants' living quarters. Compared with the lower storeys they are poor; they consist of an attic floor of small rooms with dormer ceilings, and are furnished with the simplest objects. In my bedroom, which I share with George, another footman, there are two iron bedsteads, a canvas wash-basin on a stand, and a wooden chair. Our clothes hang on pegs in an alcove. The floor is covered with oilcloth, very cold to the feet, and the window is so high that I can barely see out of it without standing on a chair.

That is a pity, for the view is very beautiful. The back of the house, where my room is situated, looks across fine lawns shaded by great cedar trees, and beyond them to the small river which is a tributary of the Bristol Avon. On the other bank are meadows in which, I am told, a battle was fought in the Civil Wars. Fortunately for Southwold village it was won by King Charles's men, who routed Cromwell's army. Had it been otherwise the Roundheads would doubtless have sacked the beautiful old church and the Family's private chapel where Talbot-Careys have worshipped for centuries.

I have never seen such grandeur as there is in the Family's rooms. The house is built in a style called Palladian, I believe, modelled on a Roman temple, with a portico of stone columns and above it a carving showing Greek men and horses. The Hall has a floor of black and white marble and a magnificent staircase leading to the upper apartments. (But the back stairs to the servants' quarters are of wood with a plain iron railing.) The rooms are immense and splendid. The walls are covered with some kind of silk and are hung with paintings which I believe are very valuable, though I hardly like to look at some of them, which display the human form very freely. In the Drawing-room the ceiling is painted with figures disporting themselves among clouds, in the same state of undress as the pictures. I suppose the nobility do not find this shocking at all, and I must endeavour to look on them as though I were used to such things. England seems to me a very free-spoken country compared with Scotland, but I do not know that we are any the better for the preachings of our Kirk elders.

Lord Southwold has given me permission to erect a bookshelf in my room on which to put Father's books and my own, though George is aye girning at me for taking up room with my possessions.

I am keeping my diary under a loose board I have discovered, for I fear George is not above reading it.

*   *   *   *

I cannot help smiling as I look back more than twenty years at the young Puritan I was. I had worked all my life among men, and unpolished countrymen at that, from whom I had heard many oaths and some tales of a very unchaste character, yet at 26 I still blushed at some of the coarse remarks made by the male staff at Southwold, particularly Pearce the coachman. Mr Widgery's language below stairs was very different from his highly correct speech in the presence of the Family. I was deeply shocked when, following him along a corridor in the wake of Daisy, one of the parlour-maids, I saw him deliberately pinch the girl on her rear, making her cry out and almost drop the laden tea-tray she was carrying. In the course of time I would come to know him as not only lecherous but cruel, both qualities I deduced from that incident.

He had, I think, some particular spite against me, whether from jealousy of my youth or because I had been given preferential treatment by Lord Southwold. It was his opinion that junior staff should be recruited from the tenants on the estate or from the village near by, as being likely to entertain a proper respect for the Family. His method of training me was to try to destroy my confidence in my own abilities, and to make my duties appear as difficult and unpleasant as possible. My first interview in the steward's room is a grim memory.

When I entered, Mr Widgery was seated at a desk covered with papers, apparently absorbed in a sum of addition. I noted that his pen was gold-tipped, and that the inkstand was a most imposing affair of pewter, covered with decoration, with the figure of a classical-looking lady playing a harp on top of it. I had plenty of time to study these details, as Mr Widgery continued to write for at least five minutes, it seemed to me, before condescending to raise his head. Yet somehow I knew that he was aware of and gloating over my deepening blushes.

'Now then,' he said at last, with a final flourish of the pen, 'let's have a look at you, young feller. Name?'

I was surprised at this, for he had known it a long time. Perhaps, I thought, his memory was bad.

'Angus Hudson, sir,' I meekly replied.

Never let me hear you say that again!' he almost shouted. 'Your name's Charles, and nothing else, while you're in this house. We don't permit fancy names for footmen.' He looked me up and down with distaste.

'Hmm. You'll have to improve your carriage before you're fit to wait on His Lordship. Straighten up, man! Keep your chin up and don't stare me in the face when you speak to me. Fix your eyes *here*' pointing to a spot somewhere about the middle of his forehead, 'and mind you do the same when addressing the Family or any of your betters. And stand up *straight*, not as if you were leaning on a fence with a sack of rabbits on your back.'

I endeavoured to adopt the stance he required. Then, having got me in position, every muscle in my neck straining with the effort of keeping still, he proceeded to recite my programme of duties, leaning back in his chair with one stout leg crossed over the other.

'You'll be up and dressed by five-thirty. Dressed for dirty work, not in your livery. You and George and Kate Bridges will get the coal in between the three of you, and it'll take you until breakfast. You'll find there are twenty scuttles to fill this time of year—twice that or more in winter.' He allowed this cheering piece of information to sink in, regarding my fallen face with satisfaction.

'Then,' he went on, 'after breakfast, which you'll take in twenty minutes and not a second more, you'll go round cleaning all the lamps and trimming the wicks, clean the candle-brackets and place new candles in them.'

What he omitted to tell me was that the candle-ends from the night before were the footman's 'perk', to be used for extra light in the bedroom. It was days before I discovered that.

'After that your next job will be cleaning the silver. Not just rubbing it up with a spit and polish, in case you were thinking of that. We make our own silver-cleaner here—Milady's very particular. Plate powder and ammonia, mixed to a cream, applied with a flannel, rubbed off when dried. And the forks done with a fork-polisher. And don't let me see any polish

114

left in the Southwold crest. If the maids are rushed off their feet with extra guests you'll help them wash and dry the glasses and decanters. When you've finished you'll change into your livery and carry the luncheon dishes upstairs. With *clean* hands,' he added, reading my thoughts as I visualised all those buckets of coal and quantities of silver-cleaner, 'even though you'll be wearing gloves. As to waiting at table, I shall take you up to the dining-room and put you through your paces' (glancing at his watch) 'now.' He rose and stood glaring at me, to my bafflement.

'Well, boy? Haven't you the manners to open the door for me?'

Scarlet-faced I did so, following his ponderous progress upstairs, across the hall and into the magnificent room where the long table, capable of being expanded with folding leaves, was already set for luncheon. In the course of the next hour (it seemed like far more to me) he gave me a training-course which reduced me to a pitiable wreck. He dinned into my head the necessity for service that was prompt but not too prompt to hurry the guests, completely silent while handling objects of such a rattly nature as cutlery and dishes, and as full of ritual as a Catholic Mass. A footman must stand to the left of a guest when serving. In removing a dish-cover he must never allow drops of moisture to fall on the table-cloth. He must sense when a guest is about to require a sauce or condiment from the sideboard, and produce it instantly. He must be able to carry a plate of soup in one hand and a dish of meat in the other without spilling either, man-oeuvring them with the dexterity of a juggler. He must never remove a dish until the last person at the table has finished that particular course, but must be hovering ready to whisk away the empty plate as soon as knife and fork are laid down at it. Before sweets and dessert are served he must be sure to remove from the table all salts, pepperettes, and unused glasses and cutlery. The instructions rattled through my head, faster and faster until they ceased to register on my brain and I could only nod feebly as though I understood.

When he had thus demoralised me, Mr Widgery put me through a cross-examination.

'Which side is wine served from? Is the label on the visible side of the bottle? How do you collect knives and forks? How do you collect *carving-knives* and forks? I am a guest requiring a second helping of vegetable. Supply one. Great Heavens, the boy's an idiot!'

As I had got every answer wrong I was ready to agree with him though I knew his hectoring had been intentional, calculated to make me feel a fool, or, as he put it, a clumsy, gawky hobbledehoy of a Scotchman, incapable of performing one action correctly. If I had been a girl I would certainly have fallen into strong hysterics, but with manly pride to maintain I set my lips and determined to exist through the tirade. Possibly he wished me to resign my post there and then; if so, he was going to be disappointed. I directed my gaze, as he had instructed me, at the middle of his forehead, reflecting what a singularly repulsive spectacle it presented, sloping greasily up to his bald crown, streaked with a few black hairs and flanked by a black tuft on either side. When he had finished raving at me, and was purple with the effort of it, I said calmly:

'Thank you, Mr Widgery. May I go now?'

He looked nonplussed; having got neither tears, rage, nor a resignation out of me, no other weapon was left to him but to dismiss me curtly.

His persecution continued steadily throughout my first week of training. Mrs Petifor, the housekeeper, paid no attention to his treatment of me. She was a placid lump of a woman, somewhat like a fat tabby-cat, with no interests beyond her household organisation and her food. From Mrs Arkwright, the cook, I think I would have got sympathy at least, but that she had a dread of 'unpleasantness' and would not risk a conflict with Mr Widgery on my behalf. She had, as I learnt, seen all new recruits to the staff equally bullied by this man who thought being a butler at least equivalent to being a Field-Marshal, even though his behaviour was that of the coarsest sergeant-major. Indeed, I had serious thoughts that week of going for a soldier after all. The life could have been no worse.

The only person to befriend me at this time was the kitchen maid, Kate Bridges, who had been with the Family very little longer than I, but long enough to sum up shrewdly Mr Widgery's character. She was a small, plump young woman with a pleasant face and a quantity of rich brown hair which she had difficulty in containing beneath her cap, earning many a reproof from Mr Widgery for untidiness.

'Only *he* called it looking like a draggletail,' she said as we washed up the glasses together; it was one of the many tasks we shared, the worst of them being the coal-fetching.

'You don't want to be frightened of him,' said Kate. 'I won't say his bark's worse than his bite, because he'd get you the sack just for the pleasure it'd give him. But you know, he's a coward underneath it all, like all bullies, and if you stand up to him you'll win.'

'That is just my own way of thinking, Kate.'

'You want to remember that he's no better than us. A sight worse, I'd say. Oh, he makes a great show of reading the Bible and preaching at us, but a girl can't go within a yard of him on her own but he grabs at her. I tell you, you won't catch me up a ladder when *that* one's anywhere around. I keep myself *to* myself, and that includes what's under my petticoats.'

'Mr Widgery's not married, then?' I asked. Kate gave a snort.

117

'Wouldn't be here if he was—no more would any of us. They won't have married staff in houses like this, for fear of all sorts of troubles. Not that *I* care,' said Kate emphatically, banging down a crystal decanter on the draining-board with alarming force. 'I'm going to work my way up in the world, and there's nothing Mr Bible-thumping Widgery can do about it. Five years from now, you won't find me slaving over the coals and the washing-up. No, indeed, I'll be out there in the kitchen, making sauces and dishes like the Family's never had.'

'Can you cook, then, Kate?'

'Cook? Me? My Mum keeps a boarding-house in Bayswater, very superior, and I've done the cooking since I was eleven years old. I watch Mrs Arkwright every minute I get, and one of these days I'll be in her place, you mark my words.'

I believed her, and was encouraged to find such bravery and determination among Mr Widgery's band of slaves.

It was a relief to me that Mother did not witness Mr Widgery's treatment of me. She had been given a room in the suite of apartments allotted to the Dowager Countess, Lord Southwold's Russian-born mother. I thought from the occasional glimpses I had of the Countess when she went driving that nobody would have guessed the relationship, with the Earl such a typical Englishman and she like an ancient fairy from a children's tale, with snowy-white hair that one could see had been as black as her eyes. Her elderly Russian maid, Madame Vilanova, was finding her duties too heavy, and was glad to have an assistant in Mother. Lily Buck, who usually helped Madame Vilanova, was absent because of the illness of one of her children, Rose and Tim. A pale, dark-haired young woman with an air of refinement about her, she was the wife of John Buck, the lodgekeeper.

Somewhat to Mr Widgery's disappointment I applied

118

myself diligently to learn my duties, making a systematic list of them and practising them at every possible moment. George gave me little or no help. To my frequent questions he replied 'Fish and find out', and other playful evasions. He struck me as far from being a model footman, making a mock of the Family and guests for the amusement of the younger staff when Mr Widgery was out of the way, and spending all his spare time at the Southwold Arms or in the barn where cock-fighting contests were held.

It was George who got me into what might have been dangerous trouble with Mr Widgery. I was feeling particularly self-confident after some days of work I knew to be well done, and hoping that I might before long be promoted to waiting at table, a duty for which I had so far been considered too raw. I greeted Mr Widgery cordially at breakfast, to be met with a stony glare. Daisy, sitting next to me at table, whispered under cover of general conversation, 'Look out, he's got it in for you,' and Kate shot me a glance of warning.

When breakfast was over Mr Widgery proceeded into battle in the hearing of several of the staff, intentionally, I was sure.

'You—Charles!' he took up a stance before the cooking-stove, where his coat-tails could be agreeably warmed while he harangued me.

'Yes, Mr Widgery?'

'Do I take it you anticipate an outbreak of war in the near future?'

I was baffled. 'War, Mr Widgery?'

'Wash your ears out, boy. I repeat, have you some secret information regarding an outbreak of hostilities? If so, it will be our duty to inform Her Majesty at once.'

He rocked up and down on his toes, smiling fatly round the kitchen in search of applause for the joke he was about to make. Mrs Petifor laid her hand upon

her bosom, exclaiming, 'Oh dear, Mr Widgery, surely
you can't mean it!' and Mrs Arkwright lingered near
the pantry door to hear the outcome. Kate, who was
noisily conveying crockery to the sink, quietened down
for the same reason.

'I do not know what you mean, Mr Widgery,' I said.

'I mean this, boy!' he whipped out from the corner
by the stove something I amazedly recognised as one
of my most precious possessions, the old broadsword
which had been taken from my ancestor Roderick
Mackenzie's dead hand on Culloden Field. Grandmother had prized it dearly, and so had I, when it
came into our possession. I had hung it on a nail on
a wall over my bed, ignoring George's derision. George,
I noticed, was not present; it was not difficult to guess
that he had curried favour with Mr Widgery by telling him of it. I felt a tide of anger rising in me.

'That is my sword,' I said. 'How did you come by
it?'

'It is my duty to know what my staff does with His
Lordship's premises,' he pontificated. 'I do not permit
the hammering of nails into walls for the display of
offensive weapons.'

'It's no' an offensive weapon!' I slipped back into
my Scots speech. 'You couldna hurt a fly with a blade
the like o' that,' and I ran my finger down its blunted
edge. 'I'll have it back, if you please.'

'But I do not please, boy!' he put it behind his
back as if tantalising a child with a toy. 'It will be
disposed of with other garbage. We musn't encourage
warmongering, Master Charles, must we? What saith
the Scripture: "He that liveth by the sword shall
perish by the sword".'

By this time my blood was fairly up. 'Give it back!'
I shouted, and tried to snatch it, aware of the feminine
flutterings from the spectators. In the struggle Mr
Widgery lurched backwards, falling against the stove.
A yell of agony proclaimed that some part of his

person had made contact with the hot-plate, and a strong smell of singeing pervaded the kitchen. Mrs Petifor gave a cry of alarm, Mrs Arkwright rushed forward to help, Daisy went into fits of hysterical laughter and Kate stood with her hand pressed against her mouth in apprehension.

Mr Widgery was stood upright and sympathised with by the two elder ladies. His face was crimson with pain and indignation. He fixed me with a savage glare.

'That's the end of you in this house, Master Scotchman!' he growled.

Kate stepped forward to my side. I could see that she was almost as angry as Mr Widgery.

'It's not fair!' she cried. 'It was all your fault because you teased him. And you've no right to keep that sword, possessions is possessions, even to servants like us.' Amid a horrified silence she held out her hand for the sword. I moved it away, saying 'No, Kate. Let it be.'

If Mr Widgery's face had been crimson before it was now a rich blackberry purple. I feared the man might have a stroke on the spot.

'Mrs Petifor,' he said grimly, 'I shall require medical attention from your cabinet of remedies. In a quarter of an hour I will see *you* two in my room.' Stiffly, with one hand beneath his charred coat-tails, he stalked from the room, Mrs Petifor fluttering behind him with little cries of alarm.

'It's the end of us, Kate,' I said. 'If only *you* were not suffering from my rash folly!'

'Walk-er!' she cried derisively. (It was a catchphrase of the day.) 'It jolly well isn't the end, Charles, or my name isn't Kate Bridges, you'll see.' And she sat down in a chair, her hands composedly folded in her lap, calmly waiting.

CHAPTER ELEVEN

When we were summoned to the steward's room for judgment we found Mr Widgery too full of wrath to engage in his usual pantomime of pretending ignorance of our presence. He at once fixed us with a baleful glare, calling to mind the Angel about to banish Adam and Eve from the Garden. The effect was somewhat spoiled by his obvious physical discomfort, for he was hardly able to sit still in his chair.

'I have no need to tell you that you are both dismissed without a character,' he said in a voice compared with which the snowy peak of Ben Nevis would be oppressively warm. 'Go to your bedroom and remove your uniform, girl. And *you* will take off that apron and return it to me together with your livery,' sweeping my person with a withering glance.

I must confess that although I had expected nothing else, my heart sank. Dismissed, in disgrace, after only a few days! Painful memories of my dismissal by Mr Rennishawe came back to me, and I cursed my evil temper which had twice led me into rash outbursts. I was about to untie my sackcloth apron and leave the room without a word; but I had not reckoned with my companion.

Kate Bridges had folded her plump arms across her bosom, as a woman does when about to embark on an argument. The red flags of battle flew in her cheeks.

'What about the month's notice, then?' she asked.

Mr Widgery snorted. 'You can whistle for it. You'll get no notice from me.'

'What about our Contract of Service?' Kate persisted. 'One calendar month's notice, it says, or wages in lieu.'

'Forfeited in certain circumstances,' Mr Widgery snapped.

'Oh, yes? Such as what? "Wilful disobedience, incompetence, neglect of duty?" You see I know the law, Mr Widgery, even if I *may* be only an ignorant working girl with nobody to protect me or take care of my rights.'

'You've forgotten something,' the butler purred. 'There is another clause dealing with Gross Misconduct, Insolence or Dishonesty. I will absolve you of the latter, but on the first two counts both you and Hudson are guilty. Now get on with you, or I'll put you out myself.'

'Try!' suggested Kate sweetly. 'You lay a finger on me and I'll scream the place down.'

He got up and advanced on her, shaking his head with rage. She neatly dodged his outstretched hands, and I stepped forward.

'You'll settle with me first,' I said. He stepped back a pace.

'Oh, go on, do!' Kate urged. 'Do, and I'll have you for assault, or my name's not what it is.'

'I—I shall call a policeman!' he raged.

'Do,' she said. 'I just happened to hear that Ted Burrows had to go to Marlborough yesterday to give evidence, and he won't be back by now unless he's grown wings. So as there isn't another policeman in Southwold it'll take you a bit of time to call one, won't it?'

The obvious truth of this daunted Mr Widgery. He growled, 'Don't give me any of your Cockney lip, my girl.' But I could see that he was weakening. Kate sidled nearer to him.

'Oh, do throw me out,' she said invitingly. 'I only want to please you, dear Mr Widgery, 'cause I know you enjoy hurting young women, don't you? And doing other things to 'em, too. I did just happen to have a long chat with Hattie Bates before she left so sudden, and she told me a lot about you, Mr Widgery. Would you like me to tell the Countess a few of the things she said, Mr Widgery?'

'You—you blackmailer!' he spluttered.

'And don't think I wouldn't dare, 'cause Milady don't like you one bit, and Milord don't either if the truth must be told, but he'd never sack you because you keep things running smooth. *She* would, though, and it would be for Gross Misconduct, wouldn't it! *Very* gross,' she added thoughtfully.

If it had been possible for Mr Widgery to flush more painfully, he would have done so: I was almost sorry for the man. Kate had battled for the right and won, and I felt it was my turn to give the wretched butler a bit of his pride back and save the situation for ourselves.

'Mr Widgery,' I said, 'I beg your pardon humbly for causing you offence, not to say injury. It was my ignorance and inexperience that led me astray. Please give me a second chance and I promise you shall have not cause to complain of my conduct. A dog's allowed a first bite before they shoot him!'

He looked at me almost gratefully, cleared his throat, and resumed his chair.

'Very well. Seeing you have apologised I'll overlook it this once. But you watch your step in future, young man. And I would advise you to read tonight in the Gospel according to St. Luke, where it is written "For whosoever exalteth himself shall be abased; and he that humbleth himself shall be exalted." You may go.' He bent over his desk, pretending to scan a letter. I had hoped to get us both out without further ado, but the irrepressible Kate asked pertly:

'Please can Charles have his sword back?'

Without a word or a look at her, Mr Widgery reached out for the sword, which was leaning against a chair, and handed it to me. As silently, we departed.

So I learnt my first hard lesson in the art of service.

Hard, but invaluable. Mr Widgery might not be a good man—indeed, he was not one—but he was a good butler, or he would have been dismissed long before for some such peccadillo as Kate had discovered, backed by the universal dislike he inspired in the bosoms of his staff. Perhaps it had been something of a lesson to him, too; he had exalted himself and had been abased, an application of the Scriptural words which no doubt never occurred to him. From that day I received many a rebuke for small misdeeds: I was told that my livery buttons were a disgrace, and that I must forfeit part of my leisure time to polishing them; I was sharply called to account for my habit of dreaming on duty, or appearing to dream; I was given menial tasks such as boot-cleaning while George escaped them. I accepted all reproof without protest, and discovered the value of dignified silence. I learnt to answer to a name which was not my own without resentment, and even to appreciate the reason for it: how could a footman ever be a Percival, an Augustus, or an Angus, for that matter?

And I put away Roderick Mackenzie's sword.

* * * *

Throughout that long late Summer, hot and airless after a heavy rainfall which perversely set in just before harvest, spoiling His Lordship's crops, I settled gradually into the ways of Southwold. After my gruelling experience soon after my arrival I had adopted the policy of listening rather than speaking, with the result that I learned a great deal about my colleagues and my employers.

I learned, for instance, that George dared not adventure beyond the borders of the estate for fear of the father of a village girl with whom he had taken liberties. Her father was said to have a trained eye and an excellent double-barrelled shotgun which was kept oiled. I learned that Her Ladyship was not pleased by Lily Buck's having brought her daughter Rose to visit the Dowager Countess, and that Mrs Petifor had been instructed to search the staircase walls for small finger-marks and the hall floor for muddy footmarks; though in fact I came to know Rose and her brother from my occasional strolls down to the lodge to smoke a pipe with John Buck and admire his flower-garden, and I found her a gentle and inoffensive child with very neat ways. I learned that Mrs Arkwright, our treasured cook, suffered from a bad back and was inclined to be short-tempered in the evening, after a day of standing up in the kitchen.

I read some of the entries in my diary for this time, and smile to see how they reflect the change in myself from a young man of hills and moors and lochs, to a denizen of the servants' hall, as interested in gossip as any old wife. Here is one for December, '81.

This evening during dinner Milady's guests were discussing the new Savoy Theatre which has recently opened in London, and the piece at present playing there. It appears that this, which is entitled *Patience, or Bunthorne's Bride*, is a musical satire upon the present school of art and literature known as the Aesthetic Movement. A Mr Oscar Wilde is a leading member of this, I hear. Strange to think that I have never yet entered a theatre, though I am most attracted to its apparent delights. A Miss Alicia Phelps who recently stayed here is, according to Miss Dawson, a highly successful London actress, and certainly was of a most striking appearance. I cannot believe that she was really wearing rouge and powder, as Miss Dawson said, but prefer to attribute the extreme brightness of her complexion to a healthy life.

The gentlemen of the party, the ladies having retired, pursued a discussion of the Irish Land Bill. His Lord-ship deplored, not for the first time, the death of the

126

Earl of Beaconsfield in April, and the lack of a strong man to lead the Tory party in his place.

'You've the cure for that in your own hands, John,' remarked his Lordship's cousin, the Honourable Cedric Markham. His Lordship laughed and shook his head. 'Too late for that,' he said. 'Always was too late. No point in wearing oneself out at the House until one's too old to enjoy retirement. Give me Southwold and peace.'

Another gentleman pointed out that 'Dizzy' had shared his time between his beloved country home and his country retreat. His Lordship replied that he would have put nothing beyond Dizzy, even to living in several countries at once. The conversation then turned to the possibility of a tunnel being built beneath the sea-bed of the English Channel, to link this country with France. It was generally agreed that this lay far in the future.

The conversation at supper below stairs was on a somewhat lower level, being on the subject of the trial of Dr Lamson for the murder of a young relative.

'Poisoning the poor little devil with a bit of cake!' exclaimed Mrs Arkwright. 'I'd like to see Doctor Murdering Lamson take liberties with any cake of mine.'

Miss Dawson snorted indignantly. 'Men will do anything, Mrs Arkwright, anything,' she said. 'Be thankful you've escaped the snare of marriage. I constantly give thanks for it.'

I heard Daisy observe to Kate under her breath that chance was a fine thing, a remark obviously overheard by Mr Widgery, who fixed the girls with a steely glance. Junior staff were not encouraged to talk at table.

'Murder!' said Mrs Petifor. 'It's everywhere. Look at this year. Poor President Garfield shot by some madman over in America. It seems only the other day that poor President Lincoln went.' (I recalled that it was, in fact, sixteen years earlier that Lincoln met his doom, but kept my knowledge to myself.)

127

'Ireland!' and Mr Widgery shook his head sadly. 'A mob of savages slaughtering each other, landlord against tenant, master against man. Why, I read the other day that the countryside round Belfast is little better than a battlefield, whole farms razed to the ground with fire and gunpowder. Shattered corpses littering the fields. Nobody is safe.' He took another large helping of cabinet pudding.

Miss Dawson shuddered. 'No respectable journal would print such outrageous things,' she said. Mr Widgery began to reply, then appeared to change his mind, and instead slathered cream over the pudding. It was well known below stairs that while airing His Lordship's newspaper in a morning, so that its sheets should not strike chill when His Lordship opened it at breakfast, Mr Widgery liked to absorb the more interesting items, reported by *The Times*, and to retail them to the staff with an air of superior knowledge.

George, who had been listening with a vacant look, suddenly spoke up. 'When I was in London I went to the Chamber of Horrors. Stayed there all afternoon. And wasn't it just a lark! There was old Mother Brownrigg a-beating of her 'prentice girl while she was strung up by her thumbs, and Mrs Manning in the very same satin dress what she was hanged in—'

'George!' roared Mr Widgery, and George subsided over his plate.

It occurs to me that in spite of the gruesome character of this discussion, and the unsuitability of murder as a topic for supper-table conversation, there is a strange fascination in the subject. Can it be that we, poor proud humans, love to sit in judgment on those of our fellows who have broken the laws and committed violence of which we would not be capable?

I put this to Lord Southwold later in the evening. We were out in the fields after rabbits, strolling amicably in the moonlight and exchanging an occasional word. My master is not a talkative man; indeed, he dislikes chatter or noise of any kind. I think that is why he is less aloof with me than with the rest of the staff, even seeking my company now and then as a companion on evening walks. I believe he thinks of me as his protégé because of his rescue of my family from eviction.

Different as are our stations, there is a sense of kinship between us; a quiet understanding which knows no barrier of wealth or class.

'Ah,' he said, when I had propounded my theory, 'you're very probably right. There's a store of violence in all of us which will out in one way or another. Innocent schoolboys gloat over penny-dreadfuls, blameless citizens go to the theatre for a merry evening of blood and thunder; every murder trial has a crowded courtroom.'

I told him of my boyhood passion for the law. He shook his head, smiling. 'Too late to don the wig and gown now, Hudson.' (In private he gave me my own name, which pleased me very much.) 'But you might find a great deal of pleasure in studying the methods of the police, which improve day by day. Quite remarkable, their ways of tracking down crime. The detective is our new fictional hero, for instance. Wilkie Collins started it, I believe. The *Moonstone,* or was it *The Woman in White* . . . ?' He drifted into silent reflection. We were now walking along the river bank. The full moon's silent reflection danced in the water, its light bathed the landscape with frosty silver. How different it is from my own land, this Wiltshire countryside with its flat meadows and willow-trees, little houses of honey-coloured stone and thatched cottages, its air sweet with the scent of cattle and stored hay. It will never be like home to me, but I feel I am settling into it, becoming in part an Englishman. There is something ancient and permanent about the countryside. Roman dead lie under our feet, flints and fragments of old armour are turned up by the plough. Who knows what ghosts walk beside my master and me?

I look back to that night from this night of the twentieth century. In the kitchen Mrs Bridges's voice is raised in anger against some unlucky person. I expect it is Sarah again. 'Never in all my born days have I seen the like of it!' she has just declared. 'Of all the idle, good-for-nothing sluts . . .' Strange to think that her voice is the voice of the young Kate of 1882, always doing battle with somebody. We were firm friends by then, and I admired her greatly, but she had not the least attraction for me. Perhaps she was too squareset. In Scotland we would have called her a sonsie quean, but I would not dare do so in England as she would undoubtedly misunderstand me.

Her ambition to become a cook was evidently looked on with favour by Providence. In the Spring of '82 Mrs Arkwright's back began to give her serious trouble. It was obvious that to remain as cook at Southwold, with all its dinner-parties and other entertainments, would turn her into a cripple for life. Reluc...ntly, and to the dismay of the Countess, she decided to retire to live with her sister at Harrogate, where she could take the medicinal baths and rest in her native air.

But before she left she asked Milady's permission to train Kate Bridges in the culinary arts, for the girl had so much promise, she said.

'A lighter hand with pastry you never saw. My mother always said it comes of having cool fingers, but there's more to it than that, M'lady. My work's been lighter, I can tell you, since Kate's been acting as cook-maid to me, and though I don't like to say it I wasn't a patch on her at her age.'

Her Ladyship, who had not the greatest patience in the world, glanced at her watch and yawned. Mrs Arkwright did not take the hint.

'For good plain meals she's as reliable as me, never

a lump in the sauce or the beef too done, and as for special—well, she can do as nice Cockeels' (as she pronounced *coquilles*) 'as you ever tasted, not to mention Filets de Sole and Grenadines of Veal with Italian Cream to follow. Your Ladyship might not believe that only last month, when my back was killing me so that I shrieked out every time I had to bend down to the roasting oven, it was Kate cooked most of that dinner for twenty-four guests, and a credit it was, I'm sure.'

I heard this dialogue (or monologue, as I should call it) as I was attending to the lamps and candle-holders. It was my impression that Her Ladyship was won over not so much by Mrs Arkwright's eloquence as by her mentioning that Kate would not, of course, expect her wage to be increased to that of a cook, £40 a year, young as she was, but would be satisfied by something about half that sum.

'Very well, Mrs Arkwright,' she said, 'you may train the girl, provided it doesn't take up too much of your time; but when you leave I shall certainly engage someone older and more responsible.'

Poor Kate, the very soul of responsibility! But she was glad enough to find her status raised and to do the work she loved. From that time Mr Widgery left her alone, for he knew that from her he would get as good as he gave, or better. She had, as Daisy said, red pepper on her tongue.

And so as good cooks go Mrs Arkwright went. Milady did not at once find a successor, so Kate cooked on with some help from a village girl as cook-maid, and threw all her heart into it. Never had the kitchen table shone so white with scrubbing, or the copper kettle beamed as though it had never seen a fire. Not one complaint was uttered at table, not one dish sent downstairs again. Kate Bridges was a happy young woman.

Happy, that is, until . . . My diary never received a

stranger entry than the following, though having read it I cannot repress a smile.

2 June, 1882

Another wet day. The farmers are grumbling in advance that the crops will be ruined.

Yesterday, Saturday, I went with Pearce to a cricket-match at Aldbury. I had never seen one before, and though baffled at first by the actions of the players, I found the game more attractive than I had expected, once I had grasped the principle of it. I intend to learn the finer points, so that I may in future enjoy the skill of batsmen, bowler and fielders simultaneously with the pleasure of fresh air and sunshine, if any.

Pearce became extremely drunk in the local inn after the match had concluded, so that I had to drive the trap home.

3 June

Seldom do I make up my diary so early in the day (it is half-past two in the afternoon), but His Lordship and Milady have gone to take tea with Lord and Lady Wilcote at Wilcote Manor, and I have a free period before me now that luncheon is cleared away.

Luncheon: I can scarcely believe it took place. The day began peacefully enough, a pleasant June morning. After breakfast I took a stroll round the greenhouses where my countryman MacPherson was tending his plants, and congratulated him on his fine tomatoes and the vine which is the pride of his heart. 'At least you're not at the mercy of the weather,' I said, sniffing with appreciation the sweet air of the conservatory, something like that of tropical climes, I imagine. Then I lingered in the Italian garden, admiring the classic Grecian temple built by His Lordship's Great-Grandfather and known as the Folly. The lake was almost covered with the delicate petals of water-lilies, pink, white and golden, plump fish of every colour swimming among them and here and there the enquiring head of a frog.

As I meditated in the welcome sunshine I saw approaching Lily Buck, pushing the invalid chair in which the Dowager Countess now visited the world outside her apartments. I greeted the old lady and enquired of Lily after my Mother's health, having heard that she had been stricken by an unseasonal attack of influenza. Then I returned to the house.

As I approached the staff door I was startled to hear loud screams from within. I hastened into the kitchen, to find Daisy holding smelling-salts beneath the nostrils of Kate, who was sitting in a chair drumming her feet against the floor and shrieking like a Ban-Shie. George and Billy the new boot-boy were standing helplessly by.

'Whatever is the matter?' I enquired when a brief pause between shrieks allowed me to be heard. They all began talking at once, until I held up my hand to stop them. Kate subsided into gasping sobs while Daisy fanned her.

'Poor dear, she can't speak,' said Daisy. 'She's had a dreadful shock—we all have. It was like this, Charles . . .'

The story she told me was incredible. After breakfast Kate had been alone in the kitchen, making out the luncheon menu. The cook-maid, Violet, was washing up in the pantry, George was about his tasks, the rest of the staff dispersed around the house. Milord and Milady had driven to the village church, as had Mrs Petifor and Mr Widgery. Suddenly the silence in the kitchen was broken by a loud crash, and Kate looked up to see that a large meat-dish had fallen from the top shelf of the Welch dresser to the stone floor, where it lay in a thousand pieces.

'Good gracious,' she said to herself, 'however could that have happened? I put it up there myself and wedged it.' She fetched a broom to sweep up the pieces, knowing that Mrs Petifor would have something to say if she found even a fragment of it left. As she swept the pieces into a central heap the broom leapt from her hands and hopped across the floor of its own volition, coming to rest against a wall. Kate gave a loud scream, unheard by anybody, for Violet was making so much noise clattering dishes in the sink while singing a hymn that she was deaf to any sounds from the kitchen.

'I thought my heart was going to stop,' Kate told me, slightly recovered by now. 'Go on, Daisy, there's a dear, while I get me breath.'

'Then,' said Daisy, 'it was like a wind come from nowhere and swept all the bits of china under the dresser. Poor Kate thought she'd gone mad, and she was making for the stairs when a great shower of potatoes come at her from the vegetable basket, like someone was throwing stones, and several of 'em hit her. Then they all fell on the floor and everything went quiet, just as I come into the kitchen.'

I looked severely upon the two young women. There had been some occasions when they had tried to lighten my supposed gravity by playing childish tricks on me (on the first of April, for instance, I received a summons upstairs which made me look extremely foolish when I realised it was what they called a jape, and on another occasion I had turned back the covers of my bed on retiring to find a basketful of the stable cat's kittens reposing peacefully beneath the blankets).

This time, however, Kate's genuine distress assured me that I was not, as Daisy would have put it, having my leg pulled. 'Pray go on,' I said.

'So I sat Kate down and made her tell me what had happened, and we both decided it could only be one of Pearce's kids playing tricks, so we hunted round for him. But there wasn't no one hidden anywhere. "Come on," I told Kate, "you've got the luncheon to cook, and that saddle of lamb's going to take some

134

time." So she set about preparing it and I went to light the gas cooker for her.'

We have, of course, the newest cooking appliances, insisted upon by Milady, who is very particular about heating and lighting. Only that winter one of *Dr. Bond's Euthermic Gas Stoves* had been installed to work in conjunction with the coal-burning range.

'When Kate had given it time to warm up, she turned round,' Daisy went on, interrupted by Kate herself.

'And it had gone out. There was no flames in the oven, just a nasty smell of gas. I thought perhaps the draught was bad and I was going to light it again when I saw the tap had been turned off. I got the shivers but I made meself turn it on and relight the burners. When I went to fetch the lamb which Violet had been dressing for me, and I went to put it in—and the stove had gone out again.'

Here she was overcome with emotion. Daisy continued the story, to the effect that eventually Kate had given up all attempts to light the stove and had placed the joints (the staff was to share a leg of mutton) in the large roasting oven of the range. Then she returned to the table and began to prepare the vegetables, asparagus and stuffed tomatoes, helped by Violet. Suddenly she felt a pressure beneath her hands, and to her horror and Violet's the table began to rise slowly, rocking from side to side. It was at this point that she had given way to hysterics, a condition in which Daisy found her shortly after I returned from my stroll.

I instructed Daisy to take Kate up to their bedroom and administer sal volatile and tea to her, while Violet and I prepared as much of the meal as we could. Later in the morning she came downstairs, pale and shaken, but able to continue her work.

In her absence we had all discussed the strange phenomena.

'She en't mad,' said Violet, 'cos I seen it too. It went up in the air like a balloon.' We all surveyed the table, a sturdy mass of deal which must have weighed as much as all of us put together. It was now perfectly still, looking as innocent as a table could.

'Ghosts,' said George. 'My Auntie had 'em in Bristol. They knocked on the walls till Auntie got the Vicar in to say prayers.'

I was inclined to agree with him, coming as I did from Highland country where fairies and phantoms were believed in firmly; but I was loth to encourage superstition, merely telling George to go about his business. Perhaps it was my presence which prevented any further disturbances. Luncheon duly appeared on the table, though I could tell from Milady's expression that she was not best pleased with it, and His Lordship remarked: 'Not quite up to standard, what?'

Nothing has been said to Mrs Petifor and Mr Widgery, of course. I do not wish any situation to arise in which any or all of us would be blamed or ridiculed.

10 June

The disturbances have now continued for a week. I am seriously perturbed and fear something uncanny is at work. On Sunday night last Miss Dawson's bed was lifted off the floor as she lay on it, and the bedclothes twitched off her by unseen hands. Her screams woke the house. His Lordship appeared among us on the landing with a candle, demanding an explanation of the noise. He is a light sleeper who becomes irritable at interruption of his slumber. We managed to pacify him with a story of Miss Dawson having had a nightmare.

At dawn on Monday three bricks sailed through the open window of the bedroom I share with George. He promptly disappeared under the bed, though no further manifestations took place. It seems physically impossible that any human hand could have thrown them so high, three storeys above the ground.

The next night Kate and Daisy were visited with loud scratchings under the floor of their room. These continued, on and off, all night, reducing the two to a state of nervous exhaustion. In the morning the rat-catcher from Bishopsbrook was sent for. He took up floorboards but found no trace of mice or rats. Nevertheless he put down poison before replacing the boards.

Kate is sure she is the target for these terrifying occurrences. On Tuesday she came running up to the dining-room as I was laying the table, frantic because a whole row of tumblers had suddenly exploded behind her, and a rush of water had poured down the chimney, extinguishing the fire.

'I can't stand it no more!' she wept with her apron over her face. 'I'm going back to London this very afternoon, that's what I am, before I get killed.'

I begged her not to weaken, reminding her that there are more things in Heaven and Earth, Horatio, than are dreamt of in our philosophy. She did not appear to take the quotation, and was only calmed by a dose of chloral taken in bed, administered by Mrs Petifor—for, of course, she and Mr Widgery could not help but hear the disturbance. I had no satisfactory answer to their enquiries, but, as I expected, was blamed as being the oldest member of the junior staff.

However, they were soon to have tangible evidence of the hauntings (for such I now admitted they were), and when Mr Widgery lifted his plate-cover to find the plate empty, but for a large toad meditating in the middle of it, he went a shade of green I have never seen rivalled even in this English countryside. Mrs Petifor was walking towards her rocking-chair at the end of the uneasy meal when it began to back away from her, finishing up against the far wall, while poor little Rose Buck, coming to deliver a message to her mother, found her hair and pinafore covered in sticky burrs, and ran crying back to the Lodge.

I did not know how we should live through that week. There was no real violence shown to anyone, merely annoyances. But who knew when they would change into violence?

'What can we do, Charles, whatever can we do?' Kate implored. 'We'll all of us be dead for sleep before long, and I'm sure my poor nerves are all of a jangle.'

'Nothing, Kate,' I said, 'unless we try prayer.' I fear none of us was particularly pious, but we turned our minds towards defeating the Devil and all his works, and I believe by Friday the nuisance was diminishing slightly.

At first we had been glad the Earl and Countess were away in London. Now I was even gladder that they were to return at the end of the week. As their carriage was seen coming up the drive an outburst of mocking laughter and a strain of wild music broke out.

'Oh, not *now!*' groaned Mrs Petifor. 'Whatever will Milady say?'

Fortunately the noise abated as they entered the house, Mr Widgery greeting them, to give him his due, with no sign of perturbation. We had agreed that His Lordship must be told, and preferably by Mr Widgery himself. That evening I happened to be in the china-closet leading off the dining-room as Mr Widgery arrived to catch His Lordship while he was in a good humour after dinner, smoking his cigar and reading a new addition to his library.

Without disrespect, I must say I was amused to hear the butler's stammering account of our extraordinary week. Though I could not see, I could imagine His Lordship's bushy eyebrows rising towards the roots of his hair. He would think he had a staff of lunatics, I reflected.

But when Mr Widgery's improbable tale came to an end, His Lordship said in a collected voice:

'All right, man, don't agitate yourself. It's only a poltergeist.'

'Polterwhat, Milord?'

'Thing that throws things about, creates disturbances,

138

some sort of uneasy spirit. Often happens in old houses, and this one goes back to 1270. Only thing to do is chase 'em off with bell, book and candle. I remember hearing—' (I heard him puffing at his cigar and blowout the smoke with satisfaction) 'round about James the First's time we had a Grey Lady on the stairs; made a perfect nuisance of herself, moaning and getting in the servants' way. But a few words from the Church and a drop of holy water soon finished her off. Poor thing,' he added kindly.

'All right, Widgery, send someone to the Vicarage and ask Mr Stonebridge kindly to step this way after Evensong tomorrow. That will be all.'

'Milord,' said Mr Widgery faintly. Later that evening I saw him returning to the house with a wavering gait and a fixed gaze. Not a man for the bottle in normal times, he had been driven to the Southwold Arms and the solace of Ben the landlord's strong ale. I, for one, did not blame him.

Today, Sunday, was particularly noisy, as if the poltergeist knew its reign was coming to an end. But we were buoyed up by hope; and after evening service Mr Stonebridge, the Vicar, duly presented himself. I heard him say, at the Earl's suggestion that the service of exorcism should be held in the Family's private chapel, 'If it's all the same to you, Milord, I would recommend holding it in the room from which the trouble seems to stem, which appears to be the kitchen.'

Milady, who was standing by, in no very good temper, broke in.

'Really, Vicar! It's quite too bad upsetting the servants like this, and I am *most* surprised at you and my husband taking this nonsense seriously. I personally have heard nothing at all.'

'Don't speak too soon,' murmured Milord. 'I think, my dear, you'd better leave this to me. Of course, Vicar, by all means hold the service in the kitchen. I'll tell Widgery to clear out the staff.'

So I shall never know what went on in that solemn ceremony below stairs. It is midnight now; the stable clock has chimed the last note of twelve. I wonder what tomorrow will bring.

11 June

The most extraordinary thing has happened. This morning all was quiet. Everybody had slept well. The household arrangements proceeded without interruption.

'It's gone,' said Kate. 'Thank the Lord.'

'I do believe it has, and just in time to prevent my health from being ruined by palpitations of the heart,' said Mrs Petifor, laying her hand on her ample bosom. One and all, we could hardly believe in the peace that had settled on us, until eleven o'clock.

Daisy had just come downstairs with Milady's coffee-tray, and was on the way to the scullery with it when a fearful burst of knocking came from the fireplace. With a shriek she dropped the tray, the smashed crockery flying all over the floor. She and Kate clung to each other. Their cries brought me up from the cellar, where I had been helping Mr. Widgery lay a case of wine that had been sent to His Lordship for his birthday. It took an hour and two pots of tea to restore the girls.

'So it's back again,' Mrs Petifor said gloomily. 'Well, I can't be expected to endure this, with my delicate constitution. I shall go to my cousin Adelaide at Weston. She's invited me often enough. Now, Kate Bridges, pull yourself together and start the luncheon. Those ducks won't last much longer, they've been hanging since Friday.'

Poor Kate gave a final sniff and struck a match to light the gas-stove. It refused to be lit. Again and again she tried, followed by the rest of us, but no flames sprang up, only a strong smell of gas.

'That does it,' said Mrs Petifor. Get off to the village, you, Violet, and fetch the plumber. Her Ladyship won't get a hot luncheon today. What have you got in the pantry, Kate?'

'There's a pressed tongue, and a side of ham I cooked Friday, and I could make a green salad if Bates will go and fetch the stuff now, and some of those little new potatoes,' said Kate. 'And I only hope it reaches the table without the roof falling in,' she added gloomily.

All was well over luncheon. In mid-afternoon Mr Ingpen the plumber arrived. I was left in charge of the kitchen, and to give him any help he needed. After dismantling as much of the stove as could be dismantled he declared he could find nothing wrong.

'Must be the mains,' he said, scratching his head. 'Though I can't for the life of me see how the flow of gas can be coming through at all if there's a leak. Never known a case like it. The only thing I can do, seems to me, is turn it off at the main and have a look at the pipe.'

As he himself had installed the stove he knew that the pipe came in under the floorboards, which had been specially laid when a section of the old stone floor had been removed to allow the gas-pipe to run from the door to the stove. He traced it to the door and beyond, then stood up, baffled.

'I can't seem to find no more of it,' he said, 'another of my chaps did the outside work, and it looks like he laid it at a tangent, as you might say. I'll have to dig a bit to find it.'

I supplied him with a fork and spade, and he went to work, whistling blithely, soon discarding his coat in the heat of the afternoon. I left him, but in half an hour or so he called me.

'Mr. Charles! I've got it. And there's something here I didn't bargain for. Hidden treasure, maybe. Let's go halves in it, eh?'

He handed to me a wooden box, stained and damp

from the earth. It was about the size of a small Gladstone bag, plain and roughly-made as though it had once held kitchen stuff. The fastening was a simple hasp.

'Let's open it up, shall us?' Mr Ingpen suggested, his mind diverted from the gas-pipe. 'Might be a hoard of doubloons and pieces of eight!' He broke into song. ' "Pour, O pour the pirate sherry, Fill, O fill the pirate glass . . ." ' I carried the box in (it was very light) and placed it on the kitchen table on a piece of sacking. Kate, fortunately, was not there to see this desecration. With Mr Ingpen's hot breath on my neck I unfasted the stiff, rusted hasp, which broke off in my hand. Together we raised the lid.

There was no treasure inside, only a quantity of small bones. We surveyed them in silence. After a pause Mr Ingpen said:

'Somebody's pet.'

'Very likely.' I picked up part of the skull. 'A tame monkey, perhaps.'

'I shouldn't wonder.' Mr. Ingpen mopped his brow, and I noted that his face no longer suffused with the glow of his toil. 'Not very pretty, is it; think we oughter put it back?'

'No,' I said. 'I believe His Lordship might be interested to see it.' On a sudden impulse I went to the stove and put a match to the burners. They ignited at once with a spurt of brilliant blue flame.

I took the box to His Lordship later this afternoon, when Mr Widgery had gone to the village. His Lordship was obviously surprised to be disturbed in his library, but welcomed me cordially.

'Forgive the liberty, Milord,' I said, 'but I thought you should see this.' I explained how it had been found, then opened the box.

His Lordship took off his reading spectacles and examined its contents carefully.

'Mr Ingpen thought it might be the remains of a

monkey,' I said. 'Ladies often kept them as pets in the old times, I believe.'

'If that's a monkey, so am I,' His Lordship replied. 'Charles, my good man, you really are a very innocent youth for your age. My grandfather kept ladies as pets, and his father before him; and not only ladies, but any females who were warm and willing. Sometimes there were—he glanced at the bones—'little consequences. Quite possibly, though it's an unpleasant thought, your "monkey" and I are related. No,' as I made to remove the box, 'leave it here. I'll have a quiet word with the Vicar.'

Tonight a very small party of us went to the churchyard after dusk, and the Vicar held a service that was not exorcism, but that for the Burial of the Dead. As he closed his book, he said quietly to Milord: 'It says here, if you recall, that the Christian burial service is not to be held over such as die unbaptised. I think I was right to make an exception, Your Lordship.'

And that was the last ever heard of the Southwold Poltergeist.

CHAPTER TWELVE

In contrast to these excitements, I have few memories of Southwold other than peaceful ones throughout that year of 1882, though the world beyond the Lodge gates was in ferment. (I have noticed that whatever the year, and however uneventful domestic life, the world beyond always *is* in ferment.) In London a madman named, I regret to say, Roderick MacLean, fired on our Queen as Her Majesty and Princess Beatrice were leaving Windsor Station. By the mercy of Providence Her Majesty was unhurt, and public thanksgiving was offered in the churches.

More happily, Prince Leopold of Albany, Her Majesty's youngest son, was married at Windsor to Princess Helen of Waldeck Pyrmont. A modern miracle was worked in the opening of the great St Gothard Tunnel, linking Northern Europe to Italy by railway through mountains previously almost impassable. The gallant men whose skill brought this about were the heroes of the hour. The magazine *Punch* presented a humorous illustration entitled *St Gothard's Tunnel; or, see the Conquering Engineero comes!* In the same pages of my own journal at this time I record Lady Southwold's exclamations of delight over a fanciful picture showing the triumphant arrival of the electric light: a chariot drawn by prancing steeds each bearing a glowing electrical bulb upon his brow, the spectres of evil and darkness fleeing before them, while in their train came a splendid pageant of fruit and flowers grown by electrical power, chickens hatched by the same, even frozen beef from Australia revived beneath its piercing rays. In the sky, an air balloon advertised itself as making the trip from

144

London to Paris in two hours, 'no sea-sickness'.

So entranced was the Countess with this that she removed it from *Punch* before His Lordship had had time to read it. I well remember his unusually sharp tones as he remonstrated with her, and her tart reply:

'Oh, bother you and your precious books and journals! The times are changing, Hugo. In twenty years everything will be lit and warmed by electricity, this damp old ruin included—you'll see!'

And of course Milady was right, as she did not fail to point out when the time came.

From the East came rumours of wars: our fleet's bombardment of Alexandria, the capture of Hanoi by the French. And of course, trouble in Ireland with that rash man Parnell and his fight for Home Rule. I shall never forget the morning when His Lordship unfolded *The Times* at breakfast, and recoiled in horror.

'Good God! Frederick Cavendish and Burke have been assassinated!'

For once the pretence that servants waiting at table are deaf to all remarks not addressed to them was abandoned. Mr Widgery (who had doubtless read the news for himself already) and I echoed His Lordship's dismay. Lord Frederick, Chief Secretary for Ireland, and Mr. Burke, his Under-Secretary, had been treacherously shot by the Fenians in Phoenix Park, Dublin, a name which will for ever remain a blot on Ireland's page of history.

'I wish the wretches would *get* their Home Rule!' exclaimed Her Ladyship. 'Perhaps we should have some peace from them if they were kept happy murdering each other. I told you what would happen when Gladstone got his hands on the reins.'

'Don't look at me, my dear,' said the Earl. 'I didn't put him in Downing Street and I heartily wish he were out of it and Salisbury there instead.' He returned to his perusal of the tragic news, while Her Ladyship opened her correspondence. The tidings contained in one of her letters caused her to frown and utter an exclamation of annoyance. She threw the letter across the table to His Lordship.

'How extremely vexing! Marjorie wants to bring that young man down on Friday. After all I've said to her.'

'What young man?' enquired His Lordship from behind the newspaper.

'Richard Bellamy, of course. I thought she had quite got over him, but it seems they're as thick as ever. Now we shall have to include him in the dinner-party on Saturday, just when I'd got the numbers right.'

His Lordship lowered his paper.

'I can't see what objection you have to him. He seems to me an agreeable young man.'

'Oh, agreeable, I dare say, but not the husband for Marjorie. With looks like hers she could have anyone she liked. That friend of Hugo's, Charles Whatshis-name, who had such nice manners when he used to come home with Hugo for the holidays—he'll come into a fortune one day. Littleton, that's the name.'

'Marjorie herself won't be exactly in want of a penny,' observed the Earl. 'I see no reason for her to marry for money. And young Bellamy may very well rise to considerable heights. Salisbury thinks well of him, I know.'

I saw in Milady's expressive face the reflection of her thoughts. It might be pleasant to have a rising young politician as son-in-law, to share in his triumphs and celebrate them in the luxurious Mayfair flat around which Milady's affections revolved. (I had heard this from Miss Dawson after she had taken an ill-considered extra glass of Christmas port.) Then her lips drooped. Richard Bellamy, at present occupying a junior post in the Foreign Office, would bring no money with him: money by her standards, that is, nor any title, unless in the course of time it pleased Her Majesty to bestow one on him.

'Really,' she said, 'with all the eligible young men in Town it's most annoying that Marjorie should have picked on this one. However, I suppose I shall have to invite him.' Her eyes wandered to me. 'He won't bring a valet, of course. Parsons' sons don't run to them.' Her voice assumed the correct tone for addressing a footman. 'You will valet Mr Bellamy this weekend, Charles.'

I bowed. It was a command I was pleased to receive. On an earlier visit to Southwold by Mr Bellamy I had been impressed not merely by his handsome appearance and manly build, but by the quality in him which I also discerned in Lord Southwold, but in all too few gentlemen of rank; perhaps it was honesty.

I was not disappointed at my second meeting with Mr. Bellamy. As I laid out his evening clothes in the second-best guest room he chatted to me as informally as if we had been two men of equal station, without patronage or condescension. He talked of his boyhood in a Norfolk rectory, of his love of reading, especially historical works; of his interest in the lives and speeches of the great age of Whig and Tory, the eighteenth century, with its rival champions, the intrepid Fox and the elegant Pitt. I, in turn, found myself talking of my own boyhood, and it seemed to me almost as if we had grown up together.

When I had equipped him for the rigours of the dinner-table he surveyed himself approvingly in the cheval-glass, and said: 'Thank you. You're an extremely good valet, Charles, from what little experience I have of valets.'

Then he turned an enquiring look on me. 'Your name is not Charles, in fact, is it?'

'No, sir. It's Angus Hudson.'

'And do you like being called Charles, Hudson?'

'No, sir. But it is part of the conditions of my employment, and I have ceased to trouble about it.'

He looked quizzical. 'Then you enjoy being a foot-man? I should have thought, somehow . . .'

'I am very happy to serve Lord Southwold, sir,' I said. 'Will that be all, sir?'

He nodded, and I left the room, seeing, as I passed the cheval-glass on my way to the door, the reflection of his deeply-set dark eyes following me.

* * * *

Several things became apparent to me during that weekend party. I saw that Mr Bellamy was deeply in love with our Lady Marjorie, and she with him, and I knew in my heart that if she were to marry him he would keep at bay those elements of character she inherited from her mother, and bring to the fore those bequeathed by her father. I saw, too, that the Earl, with thoughts of death duties and such penalties of wealth running in his head, would have preferred a son-in-law with a bank-balance as handsome as his face; but that he was ready to put such thoughts aside for his eldest daughter's happiness. Milady, on the other hand, would have willingly bribed one of the hounds to run at Mr Bellamy's horse and unseat him, if it could have guaranteed him a broken neck.

So bonny they looked, those young people, as they rode down the Countess's Walk on a bright morning, Lady Marjorie's chestnut hair a glory round her head like those I have come to accept in the stained-glass windows of English churches which my old Dominie would have thought sadly Papistical; and Mr Bellamy, so dark against her fairness, bending towards her with a look once proprietary and tender, her hand reaching out to his across the space between their horses, as though to symbolise their union.

I knew that they would marry, despite Milady and all other obstacles. I repressed a smile as I removed the tray which had borne His Lordship's nightcap of brandy and milk, on the Sunday evening before Mr Bellamy's departure. Her Ladyship was pacing up and down, disturbing the photographs and ornaments on the occasional tables, rearranging her coiffure in a mirror, and looking irritable.

'Have it your own way, then,' she said snappishly to her husband. 'Goodness knows what taxes and trouble this Government is going to bring us. We need every penny we can get, and well you know it, Hugo. If we have to sell Southwold you'll be sorry.'

'And if we have to sell the London flat *you*'ll be sorry, my dear,' he replied placidly. 'The odds are that Richard will draw you nearer to London than away from it. I intend to find him a safe seat, by the way.'

Milady raised her eyebrows. 'So! you've made up your mind. Papa gives his consent to the marriage of his beautiful only daughter to the poor but honest suitor.' She leaned against the marble mantelpiece, toying angrily with a fragile Chelsea shepherdess.

'Poor, only comparatively; honest, yes,' returned His Lordship, puffing with pleasure the last of his cigar.

Her Ladyship fired her last salvo.

'You do realise, I suppose, that he's only a Norfolk parson's son?'

'So,' His Lordship replied, 'was Lord Nelson.'

* * * *

I turn the pages to an entry which I regard with satisfaction, for it marks a great milestone in my life: the point at which my future course was determined.

15 May, 1883

The celebrations are over. After their wedding at St. Peter's, Eaton Square, Lady Marjorie and Mr Bellamy have spent two days here at Southwold in order that the estate and village should share in their rejoicings.

I have never seen a bride more radiant nor a groom more adoring; it is like a child's tale come true. Even Milady was won over, I could see, and Mr Widgery for once allowed himself several glasses of his favourite port in which to drink the happy couple's health, with the result that he had to be carried ignominiously to bed by George and myself—a difficult progress in view of the fact that George was even more intoxicated.

I maintained my usual sobriety. To me there was something a little sad about this wedding, as about others. It was the crown of a romance, the union of two healthy and beautiful young people. Never again would they be so happy or so beloved of all around them, never so hopeful, so certain that no cloud could ever roll across their skies.

And perhaps there was a touch of envy in me, too, I sensed that theirs was a happiness I should never share.

It was very quiet tonight when the last of the villagers had staggered home, the musicians had put away their instruments and left for the railway station, the Family gone to bed.

As I appeared to be the only sober person among the domestics I took upon myself some extra tasks, such as replacing the garden furniture which had been set out on the Long Terrace for such house-guests as preferred to watch the fireworks and the dancing rather than to participate. In the dusk-hidden gardens things of the night stirred; perhaps a white owl hunting, or a fox slinking towards the Home Farm. The fairy-lights strung between the trees had gone out. The only illumination visible was a faint golden glow from the billiard-room; after all, Lord Ashby and some of his friends had not yet retired. A whiff of fragrant cigar-smoke came on the night's breeze, and a young man's laughter.

I was startled almost out of my skin when somebody spoke my name from the french doors behind me.

'Oh, we frightened you,' said Lady Marjorie. We didn't mean to.' I saw her, like a white moth in some clinging robe edged with fur, hanging onto the arm of her young husband, still in evening dress. They approached me and Lady Marjorie seated herself on one of the cane chairs, pulling down Mr Bellamy to the one beside her. I looked at them in some puzzlement, for I felt that they had come on purpose to find me.

'Shall I fetch you a wrap, Lady Marjorie?' I asked. 'The evenings are chill at this time.'

She smiled and shook her head. 'You think I'm indecent, Charles, don't you, but I'm really quite respectable. These peignoirs are all the rage, you know.'

'Really, my dear!' protested Mr Bellamy. How often would I hear him say those words in years to come, with more affection than reproof in his musical voice.

'We came down to have a word with you, Charles,' he said to me. 'Lady Marjorie thought it would be more informal than a summons to the morning-room or the library.'

'Sir?'

Mr Bellamy cleared his throat. 'We have not often met, Charles, have we?'

'No, sir.'

'But often enough, I believe, for me to form my own judgment of you and you of me. Now, would you say I was the kind of employer of whom you would approve?'

'I would not presume, sir.'

'Oh, don't be stuffy, Charles,' put in Lady Marjorie. 'You sound more like eighty than twenty-eight or whatever it is you are. What my husband is trying to say, only he'll be Parliamentary and flowery about it and take all night (no, Richard, I *will* go on), was that he's come to think very highly of you, not only from observations but from what Papa says about you.'

'May I speak, my love? As Lady Marjorie says,

Charles, I feel you warrant a more responsible post than that of a footman. I feel, as it were, that you *need* responsibility. Do you agree?'

I thought. 'Yes, sir, I think you are right.'

'I believe, Charles, that you have an ideal of service which is very rare today; that you have what in religious circles would be called a vocation for it. Do you understand me?'

'Yes, sir.'

'Perhaps you remember—no, you probably don't—but one of the old poets expressed it rather well in a verse about the willing servant who 'makes drudgery divine; Who sweeps a room as for Thy laws Makes that and th' action fine.'

I did not recognise the quotation; I wished I had. 'My reading has been somewhat limited, sir,' I said, 'but had I come across that sentiment I should have thought it very true.'

'What my husband is trying to say, Charles,' said Lady Marjorie gently, 'is that when we move into our new home in Eaton Place, Mayfair, we shall need staff. One can get maids and things from the servants' agencies, of course, but we do need a good, reliable butler, somebody we know and can trust. Will you come and buttle for us, Charles?'

I do not know what I replied, though it was a mere hour ago. I believe I must have appeared stupid, for they both had to repeat the offer before I could fully understand it. I know that I stammered something about His Lordship, and Mr Bellamy assured me that Lord Southwold was aware that they wished to make use of my services, and had given his blessing. Then, so far as I recall, I said that I would be only too happy, and even made a small speech about it; after which they both shook hands most cordially with me.

'You will be a very young butler,' said Mr Bellamy, 'but then we are a very young couple, so nothing could be more fitting.' We shook hands again; and they turned to go.

At the french doors Mr Bellamy paused, looking back at me.

'Good night, *Hudson*,' he said.

16 May

My astonishing news, which I could not keep to myself, was received below stairs with mixed feelings. The ladies were on the whole pleasant about it. Mrs Petifor averred that never, in all her born days, had she seen a young footman elevated to such grandeur, but that I was a hard-working and respectable person who knew his place in the world.

Daisy exclaimed, 'Lor! Well, fancy!' and went off into peals of giggles. She has not been able to address me all day for giggling. Kate congratulated me warmly and even placed a sisterly kiss on my cheek. I appreciated this, for I knew from my own observation that Kate was less happy with Mrs Amey than she had been with Mrs Arkwright, and that her brief spell as Cook had given her a taste for working to her own rules rather than to another woman's.

But upon the men my tidings had a very different effect.

Mr Widgery did not even trouble to hide his disgust at my appointment. All his original dislike of me returned and expressed itself forcibly. When I broke the news to him he uttered not a word, but turned on his heel and stalked away from me. Kate met him a few minutes later coming away from His Lordship's study, and we guessed that he had been to enquire whether I had been telling the truth, and if so to lodge a complaint. I know that for the rest of my service at Southwold I shall lead a dog's life.

George was scarcely more pleasant. I could see that he was bitterly jealous. 'Going up in the world, are we? We didn't never carry coal upstairs, nor clean the silver, did we? Sixpence to speak to us now,' and in this jeering manner he continued all day.

At dinner-time he went further. As I was proceeding towards the stairs with a tureen of soup, George, who was sitting by the kitchen table, suddenly put out a leg and tripped me. I fell heavily, injuring my arm, and the tureen (fortunately not one of the monogrammed set) flew into a thousand pieces and distributed soup in every direction.

George laughed heartily. Not so the ladies; Mrs Amey cried out in horror and Kate ran to help me up. My coat was ruined, my arm felt as if it had been broken, while stars danced before my eyes from the force with which my head had hit the ground.

'You did that deliberate, George Spink!' cried Kate. 'I saw you, with my own eyes!'

'Prove it, then,' he retorted. Kate gave a snort of disgust and set about cleaning up the mess, while Mrs Amey scuttled about for another tureen and fresh supplies of soup. I nursed my aching head and bruised arm, and trusted that George had now vented his spite and would leave me alone.

17 May

My hopes were dashed. After a day of petty insults from Mr Widgery, and the allocation to me of menial tasks on the plea that George was suffering from a severe headache (if he was, it did not interfere with his reading the *Sporting Times* in bed) I returned to the bedroom which we unhappily share to dress for dinner. My own head was still aching from last night's fall, and I was stiff and sore, but nothing, I was determined, should prevent me from waiting at table, particularly as a dinner-party was to be held, in order that the nobility of the county should be introduced to Lady Marjorie's husband.

I managed painfully to don my livery, which Kate had cleaned with petroleum. Then I opened the drawer in which I keep my Father's gold half-hunter, a treasured legacy on which I rely for the correct time when serving at table. It was not there. The case in which it is stored during the day was empty. I searched hastily among my few possessions, then addressed George.

'Have you seen my watch? It appears to be missing.'

'Search me. Go on, look in all me pockets. I'm honest, ain't I? I don't fear nothing.' Grinning, he returned to his newspaper.

I searched his pockets, his drawer, even his box of clothes and other effects, in vain. Then I concluded my dressing and went down to carry out my duties, with a black suspicion in my mind.

It was the goddess Coincidence, I feel sure, who ordained that I should be within sight of the steward's room after supper that night. I saw George come out, in conversation with Mr Widgery, both appearing to be enjoying a joke; and I saw Mr Widgery pat his pocket as if reassuring George of something.

The Highland blood in me on very rare occasions gives me the Sight. I knew at once where my watch was, and what was to be done with it; and when Mr Widgery emerged later, clad for outdoors, I followed him.

Out through the gardens he went, myself treading softly behind, as I had learned to tread when I was a gamekeeper's son. Before the lodge is reached there is a dark coppice in the footpath from the house. It was there that I pounced on Mr Widgery from behind, and had the pleasure of hearing his bleats of terror, as I got a stranglehold on him.

'Where is it?' I asked.

'I don't know what you mean. Let go!'

'Not until I get my watch back.'

'I don't know anything . . .' I tightened my grip on his thick neck. 'I think you do,' I said. 'How do you like this grip? I have used it on poachers with marked success.' Choking, he pointed to his coat. 'Waistcoat,' he gasped. 'Inside pocket.'

And there, sure enough, was my dear Father's watch. I took it and let the thief fall where he lay, rubbing his throat in the shade of the laurels.

He will not trouble me again, I believe.

* * * *

Fortunately for me, it was only a month before I was told that Lady Marjorie and Mr Bellamy had moved into their London home, and that I was required at once. My possessions were few, my friends even fewer; there was little preparation to be made. Mother, whose health had been steadily failing during the past year, had been relegated to a small and poorly-furnished room since she had no longer been able to wait on the Dowager Countess, and was low in spirits as well as in health. Happily, a letter to Fiona, who with her husband was running a small lodging-house at Folkestone, produced an offer to accommodate Mother for as long as she wished.

I saw her off on the London train a few days before my own departure. She looked very small and frail, though her spirits had risen since the good news of Fiona's welcome. She kissed me, then held me at arms' length, searching my face fondly.

'Father would have been prood of ye, Angus. 'Ye've aye gone yer ain way, and it's the only one for you, even though it's not the way ye wanted.'

It was on my last day of service at Southwold that I received a piece of grand good news. Kate, her sensible face for once flushed with emotion, came to me like one bearing a secret.

'How will you like going to London alone?' she asked.

'There would be little use in my *not* liking it, Kate,' I replied.

'Trust you to say something like that! Well, I hope you'll be pleased to hear that I'm coming with you. Lady Marjorie asked for me special—as her cook.'

I was delighted, of course, to be taking a friend with me on the journey to my new life; a friend who at the other end of the journey would become Mrs Bridges, as I became, for all time, Mr Hudson.

* * * *

It is twenty years and more since that day. Mrs Bridges, unmarried but bearing a cook's courtesy title, has grown plumper and greyer, but has lost not a morsel of her good sense and good temper, not to mention her surpassing skill in cookery. And I? In my fiftieth year, scantier-locked than I was, I am proud to be known among Lady Marjorie's acquaintances as the Perfect Butler. I rule my staff more humanely and fairly, I trust, than did Mr Widgery, who has long since gone to his reward. If I am not loved, I am respected and, I believe, liked by one or two.

I have my hobbies, serious-minded though I am. I have learnt to enjoy cricket-matches and to take an interest in the great contests fought beween England and Australia for the 'Ashes', a humorous name arising from a facetious obituary notice for English Cricket in the *Sporting Times*. I have watched the three great Grace brothers of Gloucestershire, the elegant Hayward, those magnificent left-handers of Yorkshire, Peate, Peel and Rhodes, the famous partnership in 1898 between Brown and Tunnicliffe. In the winter I spend some of my leisure time in studying the skilled players of Rugby football.

On an evening when my duties permit, I sometimes attend the theatre, which I enjoy more for the absence of distracting companionship; or I take a cup of tea or a glass of beer with my friend Sergeant Williams, of

Gerald Row Police Station. It is the nearest I have ever come to the Law.

I have seen servants come and go at 165 Eaton Place; one still with us is my head house-parlour maid, Rose, who is none other than the little girl Rose Buck who lived at the Lodge of Southwold. I have seen my employers, Lady Marjorie and Mr Bellamy, in times of joy, such as the birth of Miss Elizabeth and Mr James, and in less happy moments. I have watched the career of Mr Bellamy from a modest young man in the Foreign Office to the post of Under Secretary of State at the Admiralty. I am still proud to serve them both.

But for a slight colouring in my voice (Sergeant Williams, a Welshman himself, has alluded to it as a sniff of old malt whisky) strangers would take me for an Englishman. When I travel to Scotland with Mr Bellamy in the grouse season it is as a stranger that I revisit her, and I am glad to return to Eaton Place and the familiarities of everyday life.

Yet my memories are real to me still, as I turn over these pages of faded ink: Donald and I fishing for trout, my Grandmother's tales of Highland glory, great cloud-shadows moving over the smooth face of Ben Lomond, a rosy flush of heather spreading over him in Autumn; a gold earring on the ground; a terrified hare in a trap; and Lindsay's eyes.

Looking back over the pages, I see that I have written down a verse from a Scottish exile's song:

'Sing me a song of a lad that is gone;
    Say, could that lad be I?
Merry of soul he sailed on a day,
    Over the sea to Skye.'

How does it continue?—

'Give me again all that was there,
    Give me the sun that shone;

Give me the eyes, give me the soul,
    Give me the lad that's gone!'

A voice has broken into my musings, calling stridently from the kitchen; the voice of Mrs Bridges.

'Mr Hudson! Mr Hudson! The dratted chimney's got itself on fire!'

With something between a smile and a sigh, I close the chronicles of my youth. Back into the darkness of their box, never, perhaps, to be read by any eye but mine, go my diaries.

All Sphere Books are available at your bookshop or newsagent, or can be ordered from the following address:

Sphere Books, Cash Sales Department,
P.O. Box 11, Falmouth, Cornwall.

Please send cheque or postal order (no currency), and allow 7p per copy to cover the cost of postage and packing in U.K. or overseas.